On The Edge Of The Storm

His Stormchasers
Book 2

By

Ronna M. Bacon

Nahum 1:7 The Lord is good, a stronghold in the day of trouble; he knows those that take refuge in him.

Table of Contents

Prologue

Her eyes darting around, the young woman searched the darkness, feeling hunted and haunted and chased. She clutched the papers in her hands, not sure what she had, and ran for her bedroom, slamming the door before she slide to the floor, her back to it, her hands tight on the paper. He had found again, she thought.   All her hiding, moving from town to town, hadn't worked. He was out there. He had been in her home, once again.

She stared at the papers she held, a frown on her face.   Now what, she thought?   She flipped through them quickly and then more slowly, her heart sinking.   This is not what she had expected, to see evidence of the crimes he was involved with.   She needed to get them to someone but who? And how?

She finally rose, the apartment dark, and felt her way to her desk, searching for a large envelope and sealing the papers inside, setting them with her purse. Tomorrow, she would find someone she could talk to, someone who would understand.

The man stared at her the next morning, then at the envelope, before he reached for it and took it, his questions causing her to shake her head and rub her hands together as she sat at his desk, her eyes on the envelope as he opened it.

Keen eyes searched through the material before he looked up and beckoned someone else over, their conversation muted.   She listened, not quite understanding what they were saying until the first man looked at her and nodded.

He told her this was what they had been looking for, that they would be able to arrest the man and charge him. She shook her head as they asked her to stay, rising and almost running from them, leaving them standing staring after her.

She kept in contact, working with them, until one day she looked up and saw the man in front of her, his hand reaching for her. She turned and ran, ran for her apartment, grabbing the knapsack she kept packed at all times, and then scurrying down the back stairs and out of the building, heading for where, she wasn't quite sure, just knowing she had to escape.

Days passed, and she grew thin, looking over her shoulder, not seeing him but knowing he was around. She finally found what she hoped and prayed was a sanctuary, a little home on the shores of the lake. She stayed there, not moving around much, praying that he hadn't found her but knowing that somehow he would. He always did.

Chapter 1

The cold wet wind blowing in from Lake Erie drove directly through the ragged jacket Reilly Stuart wore, finding its way through the ratty and torn sweatshirt to his flesh. He shivered, squinting at the moon. Two in the morning, he thought, as he directed his gaze at the lonely beaten cottage he had finally found. The lady he had been searching for the past five weeks, no, six, he corrected himself, was inside. He had finally found her. She had been out briefly before midnight and he caught the sight of logs in her arms. He shivered again, wishing he was somewhere warm and dry. Standing under trees near a shoreline just didn't cut it anymore. And just why had his father decided it would be him to bring her in?

He hadn't had to pull out the tattered photo he had tucked into a pocket. After all those weeks, he didn't need it to know he had found Aideen Fletcher. Just why she had run all those months ago, he didn't know and frankly really didn't care about. All he knew was that they had been hired by her brother to bring her home.

Reilly's thoughts turned to the man older than himself by ten years or more, but that was hard to tell. Adam Fletcher had the look of someone who lived hard, partied hearty, and didn't care about the consequences. The question that had been tickling at the edge of his mind resurfaced. Why did he even care that his sister had left, leaving her work, her house, her friends, her parents? Reilly had always felt uncomfortable with the explanation that Fletcher loved his sister and just wanted to know she was safe.

He turned as he heard a cautious footstep and a branch snapped under a heavy foot. He heard the muffled curse at the noise and squinted through the darkness, lit only by the light of a half moon. He sighed. He had been followed after all. Now what, he wondered. Lord, I could sure use some help here. I need to keep her safe and get her away. I've always had the feeling someone's been dogging my steps. I guess I was right after all. So, Lord, where do I go from here?

He shoved away from the tree, taking advantage of a cloud briefly covering the moon and making his way to the back door of the cabin. He had already circled it numerous times. This time, he would have to enter and convince the lady she needed to go with him.

He felt for the door knob and twisted it, not sure what he would do if it was locked. It turned under his hand and the door opened. He slid inside, standing back to the door, letting his eyes adjust to the dim lighting, feeling the welcome warmth from the fire. He heard a whisper of movement and ducked, the fireplace poker just missing his head. He dove for the lady, taking her down, wrapping his arms around her and tucking his head down against her neck as she fought him. His words had no effect on her.

Aideen Fletcher was panicked. Adam had found her, after all that time. She knew her days were numbered. After what she had done, he wouldn't let her live. Not a chance. He may be her brother, but he had no love for her. In fact, he had delighted in tormenting her all her life, playing the innocent when their parents intervened. She had come to realize that no matter what she said, they were always on Adam's side. She had left home at eighteen, moved to a smaller town across the province, and then finding evidence of his crimes, had turned him into the police.   He had vowed revenge on her.

Now, as the man's weight took her to the floor, she struggled even harder.   Then his words finally made their way through her panic and desperate need to escape. She stilled, her hands on his arms that she had been pushing against.

"Thank you." Reilly's breath came in gasps. "I'm not your enemy. I was hired to find you and bring you back."

She turned, and he caught the clear gray of her eyes in the dim light, eyes that went so well with her dark brown hair. She shook her head.

"I can't go back!" There was desperation in her voice. "He'll kill me if I do. He promised to do that."

Reilly sat up, his hand helping her to do the same. "Why?"

"Because he said he would." She crawled away from him, using the armchair to pull herself up before she sank into it. "I turned him in and he said I would live to regret it." She gave a hoarse laugh. "No, then he said I would die to regret it. What brother does that?"

Reilly stared at her. What she had just said didn't match with what they had been told. He sighed. He needed to talk to his father, head of their recovery business, and get his answer. He had been out of touch for four weeks now, not daring to contact any of his family.

"Why would he say that? He told us he was concerned because you had left without any word to the family."

She snorted, causing his brown eyes to narrow. "Yeah, well, you'd do the same if you were being stalked by his cohorts in crime, finding your home destroyed time after time, your vehicle vandalized. I had no choice."

Reilly's head turned suddenly as he heard footsteps near the front door and dove for her, shoving her to the floor as the doorknob twisted. He spun and headed for the back door, clicking the lock into place, but knowing the doors would not hold anyone out for long.

"Where are the bedrooms?" She stared at him. "The bedrooms? They have windows big enough we can get out of?"

She finally nodded, was on her feet, and grabbing for a jacket and a knapsack hanging beside it before she headed for a room.

"In here. This window opens out into some brush. I should have cut it back but kept it tight to the house, just in case of something like this."

Reilly followed her out of the window, dropping silently to the ground, and then grasping her hand, led her on a run to the trees. Hearing shouts behind them, he pulled her faster with him. She tugged at his hand, trying to steer him to another path. He took it, looking briefly over his shoulder. The men were back there, he could tell.

"Where now?" Reilly stopped them, and then had her down on the ground as he heard the familiar sound of shots being fired at them.

She looked around and then pointed. "In there. There's a huge deadfall. I took a look at it yesterday, planning on using it for hiding if I had to." She pulled him to his feet, ducking under branches as she led the way. "In here. We can hide, at least until morning."

"I don't think morning will make any difference, darling." Reilly shoved her in first and then followed, his eyes and thoughts on the men after them, not catching her look of surprise at the word he had used.

They heard the men stomping back and forth, the loud conversation, the curses, the sounds of the night stilled by the commotion. Aideen finally laid her head on his back and slept, exhaustion taking control of her body. Reilly shifted slightly so he could wrap an arm around her and at least try to keep her warm. He watched through the remaining hours, a fine anger beginning to burn inside him.

A setup, he thought. A setup to find her. We were used. Somehow, I need to get in touch with Dad or Rory and let them know what happened. It's not safe to take her in. He sighed. There goes my plans for a nice home cooked meal with my family, clean clothes, and warmth.

Chapter 2

Looking around as dawn crept into the eastern sky, chasing away the dark of the night, Reilly listened to the awakening sounds of the woods and wished circumstances were different. He looked back at Aideen, finding her still curled up against a root and asleep, and shook his head. Who was telling the truth, he wondered, Aideen or her brother? His money was on Aideen, but he had to have proof, proof his father would require. And at the moment, he had no way of getting that.

Aideen stirred, her hand brushing back her hair, as she sat upright and stared around, glaring at Reilly's back. No, she thought, it's not his fault. Adam played his cards well. He's convinced them he's really concerned. Only he's not. Last night, or this morning, whichever it was, proved that very fact. She watched as Reilly turned slightly, a small smile crossing her face as he grinned at her.

She took in his brown eyes, brown hair, and shook her head. No, she thought. Not again. I went that route years ago. I found someone I thought I could love, and Adam ruined it. Never will I let him have a chance to destroy that.

Reilly finally rose, his hand reaching to help Aideen out. She pulled hers free as soon as she had cleared the roots, stuffing both hands into her pockets. She looked around and then turned to walk back towards the path, coming to an abrupt halt as Reilly snagged the back of her jacket and stopped her.

"Just what did you do that for?" Anger laced her words.

"I go first." Reilly stared at her before she finally looked down. "I go first, not because I don't want you to. I go first because I need to make sure you are safe."

"I'm not going back, Stuart. Get that through your brain. I'll run again." The words were spit at him.

He pulled her back behind him. "I go first. I don't care what you say. And no, you're not running. I won't let you."

"You won't let me? Since when?"

"Since last night when I walked into the cabin." He turned, a quick grin on his face. "You have a nasty swing there. You almost nailed me with that poker."

She shook her head. "I'm sorry. I thought it was Adam or one of his goons."

"Goons? Who talks like that?"

"I do." She shoved at his back. "Let's go. I want to go back to the cabin, grab my stuff and find somewhere else to hide."

Reilly stared at her for a moment. "I'm sorry, Aideen. We can't go back there. I doubt there is anything of yours left now, anyway."

"What are you talking about?" She stared at him and then spun to stare towards the lake, seeing smoke drifting through the air. "They didn't, did they?"

She shoved at him and was running back down the trail before he realized what she was up to. He raced after her, taking her to the ground, and finally have to pull an arm behind her to stop her fighting.

"It's too late, Aideen. They'll have burnt the cabin. Likely as a warning to you."

He felt her body stiffen and then begin to shake as the sobs started. He gave a groan. He wasn't good with ladies' tears. His two sisters always told him that. He shifted to a sitting position, and then pulled her into his arms, holding her until the sobs subsided. She just sat then, her head resting against him before she took the handkerchief he offered.

She stared at it. "A handkerchief? What man carries a handkerchief nowadays?"

"Lots of men still do. Mom drilled it into our heads we had to, so we do. We know better than to cross her." He gave a small smile at a memory.

"Did they really burn the cabin?" Her voice was quiet, so low he had to bend to hear her.

"I think so. Did you have anything else there?"

She shook her head. "Everything I own is my backpack." She sighed. "Can we at least go and look?"

He helped her to her feet, keeping her hand tight in his. She looked askance at that and then at him. He ignored her looks, intent of searching the area around them. He stopped short of the edge of the trees, hearing men's voices and held a finger to his lips. She nodded, and then walked with him as near the edge of the trees as they could get without being seen. She shuddered at the devastation. The fire had taken the cabin, leaving nothing but some logs and ashes.

Reilly felt her hand on his arm, the fingers digging in. I'll have a bruise, he thought, then looked around. He pointed to a stump and moved her there.

His mouth close to her ear, he spoke. "Wait here. I'm going to wander out and see what I can find out." He smiled at the mutinous glare on her face. "I'm not going until you agree to wait here. I need to know I can trust you, that you won't run." When she didn't answer, he sighed. "Aideen, I need you to work with me on this. I need you to trust me. I believe you." Her eyes shot to his at that and he could see a tiny spark of hope flickering in their depths. "I do believe you. But to convince my father and the others, I need to have proof. Let me work with you on that. Find the proof we need, and then we can go in."

"You believe me?" Her voice was quiet, uncertainty lacing it.

"I do. I never felt comfortable with what your brother was saying. And the men he had with him? Dad pegged them as guns for hire. If your brother is on the up and up, why would he have protection like that?"

"Because he's not on the up and up. I have proof, but I can't get to it. Not if he's following me." She shivered, not from the cool morning but from fear.

"Aideen." Reilly looked around, hearing the fire trucks leaving. "We'll wait. I doubt the men will be back, but they may have hung around, thinking you would come out into the open and they could grab you."

She shrank back, fear once more colouring her face. "They will be here, somewhere. I can't go out there. And you can't. They'll know it was you."

"Not likely. They will have an impression of my build, but they won't have seen enough to know me." He looked around and then reached to pull her to her feet, not releasing her hand as he walked them rapidly back the way they had come.

"Stuart, you're going the wrong way. We need to go out by the cabin." She tried to pull him back that way.

He shook his head even as he sent her a grin. "No. I came in this way. I left the truck I've been using back here." He stopped. "Or at least I had. It's gone."

"I hope it wasn't worth a lot. I could have told you there were a lot of vehicle thefts." She smirked as he narrowed his eyes at her.

"You could have, huh?" He walked towards the road, dropping to a knee to study the footprints. "Two. Likely the men from last night." He rose, a hand rubbing down his cheek. "There goes our transportation. How are you at walking?"

She shook her own head and started off, only to have him reach out a hand and stop her. "Aideen, we need to set some rules."

"And why would that be?"

"Because as of now, or last night I guess, you're in my custody." He pulled out his identification, her face paling as she read it. "I can protect you as best I can, but I need you to work with me. First, I need to find a phone and call in."

"And let them know you have me? I don't think so." She shoved at him and then took off at a run.

He stared after her, shook his head and set off at a rapid pace, his arm coming out to wrap around her and pull her to a stop. She struggled, but he just stood still, taking the hits from her before her body sagged against him.

"I promise, I won't let him hurt you. You've convinced me. I can convince my Dad. God has us, you know. He is right here."

She snorted at that. "God? He doesn't care about me. If He did, I would not be running for my life." She shoved at his arm and this time he let her go. She spun, anger on her face. "Don't tell me God cares. He gave up on me years ago."

Reilly was saddened by her words, by the defeat in her body, by the anger, by the hurt she had suffered. He could only think of his own two sisters and be grateful they had never faced what she did.

He reached for her hand and pulled her with him to the side of the road, before turning them to walk towards town. He let her be silent, talking idly about his family, what he had seen over the last month, his eyes watchful.

He suddenly shoved her behind some bushes and crouched down beside her. She turned on him, ready to tell him off, when she heard the vehicle. She paled. She knew the sound of that vehicle, the engine had a tell-tale noise to it. She clutched at Reilly, pointing out there before she leaned close, her voice a mere whisper.

"That's Adam's car. Isn't he in jail?"

Reilly shook his head, even as he looked around. "No, for some reason, he's out. Dad was looking into that but I haven't spoken to him in a month."

"A month? Why?"

"Because I was tracking you. I had to play a part and cell phones didn't fit. If I had really needed to talk to him, I'd have found a pay phone." He smirked at the look on her face. "They still have some. You know, those old-fashioned phones you have to put money into before you can dial?"

"I know that. I'm just surprised you've been out of touch." She stopped speaking as she heard the footsteps approaching. Reilly shoved her down even further and then used his own body to cover her, an arm wrapped around his own head.

He listened to the conversation, picking up few words, but enough to know they were being sought. He sighed. Lord, just what did You go and do with me? I'm only supposed to find her and bring her back. Now, I'm on the run and it's up to me to keep her safe.

Chapter 3

Reilly pulled Aideen off into the wood mid morning, gently shoving her down to the ground and looking around. They should be coming into town soon, but he was really uncomfortable with Aideen doing that, not when the men were still around. He sank down beside her, his arms resting on his upraised knees as he listened.

"We're only about fifteen minutes from town, Reilly. Why did you stop?" Aideen was puzzled.

"Because I don't want you going into town, not yet. I want you to stay right here, hidden, and I'll go in, grab some supplies, and a cheap phone, and be right back." He could tell she didn't like that but they really had no choice.

She finally nodded, looked around and moved further back from the road. Reilly could tell she was exhausted, not just physically. His mood darkened and he had to pray hard to release his burden for her. How a brother could treat a sister that way was beyond him. He and his two brothers had teased and tormented their two sisters growing up and had been teased and tormented in return, but when it came right down to it, they looked out for each other.

He waited for a few minutes and then took off on a run, knowing he didn't want to leave Aideen there for long on her own. He quickly found food and water, found a cheap phone that he had charged while he was shopping for other supplies. Heading back towards the edge of town, he made a detour. His own truck was still where he had stored it. He quickly pulled away, eyes watching, not seeing anyone.

He stopped on the shoulder of the road near where he had left Aideen. Locking his truck, he searched for her, finally finding her hidden deeper in the woods.

"Aideen? What happened?"

"There seemed to be a lot of traffic and I heard Adam's car again. I can't get caught, Reilly. I can't. He'd kill me. That's what he wants me for. To torture and then kill me. God help me, I need to get away."

Reilly stared at her, shocked for the moment, and then reached and gently guided her to his truck, shoving her into the passenger seat and then running around to climb in himself. He took off, not sure where he was heading but knowing that somewhere along that shoreline, he would find a place for them to hole up. He had to. Aideen needed a proper place to rest and he needed somewhere he could crash. He also needed to contact his father. He had a bad feeling in his gut that something was about to break loose and he needed to protect the lady with him.

He walked her to the truck, opening the door, hand out to help her up. She stared at the seat and then back at his hand, fatigue weighing even that movement. He gave a sigh and then lifted her in.

"Seatbelt, Aideen." He watched as her head went back on the seat and then reached for the seatbelt himself, securing her in before he closed the door, standing with a hand on it, his eyes searching the area. He could feel something or someone and he wanted out of there as quickly as he could. The sounds of the woods had died away. He moved quickly to round the truck and slide behind the wheel, driving slowly away, his eyes moving from side to side and then to the rearview mirror. Nothing. No one. But he knew someone had been there. Friend or foe, he had no idea which.

He finally found a rest stop, overlooking the dark and angry waters of Lake Erie, and undoing his seatbelt, reached behind him for the bag with the food. He handed Aideen a bottle of water, and when she didn't open it right away, reached to unscrew the cap.

Aideen was puzzled. Why, she asked herself, was he treating her like a lady? Not one man in her life ever had before. Certainly not her brother. Her father had had no time for her, too busy with his real estate empire as she sneeringly called it. God, He didn't care. She had come to that conclusion months ago, when Adam had showed up, threatening her through the locked and bolted door to her apartment, his words slurring from the alcohol he had consumed. She had slid to the floor, back to the wall near the door, her arms wrapped around her head, trying to avoid hearing the names and slurs he was sending through the door. At that point, she knew she had to run. Watching from the window as he drove away, praying that he would be pulled over and jailed for impaired driving, she had then run for her bedroom, stuffing what little she wanted to keep into a backpack and then running for her car.

She had driven quickly away, not seeing the vehicle following her. She had driven for hours until fatigue caused her to find an out-of-the-way motel. She had stayed there for a night and then, driving away, she found what she had been looking for. A quick stop at a used car lot and she had no vehicle. The salesman had been kindly, had offered her a ride, but she had shaken her head, stating that she would be staying in town for a while, and where was the best place to get a meal? She laid the groundwork, or so she hoped, that she was planning on staying where she was. In all reality, her mind was racing. She headed for town, stopped for a quick meal, and then searched for the store she wanted.

She found a room to rent by the day, knowing she didn't want to commit to a week or a month. She changed into the ragtag clothes she had found in the thrift shop and then hit the streets, her backpack on her back, a toque with her hair tucked up under pulled down as far as she could on her face. She headed for the bus station, pushing at the glasses she had found in a drugstore, hoping they would change her looks.

She had wandered the southern portion of her home province of Ontario, not sure where to go that Adam wouldn't find her. About two weeks ago, she had settled in the little cabin, using an alias. The woman had looked askance at her, agreed to accept cash from her for three weeks, and then handed Aideen the keys. Aideen knew it was a walk to get into the small town, but she felt safe. That was, until Reilly had shown up last night. Now the cabin was gone, she was missing, and the police would be after her to answer questions.

She shot Reilly a swift look before she reached for the opened water bottle. She drank a bit and then screwed the top back on. She looked down at his hand, handing her a sandwich he had just concocted before she looked back at him.

"Eat. The fixings are fresh and good. I didn't want to take a chance on any vendor sandwiches." He shoved it at her, and she grabbed for it before it fell onto her lap. "Drink. There is plenty of water. If you don't want water, there are some juices. I wasn't sure which you preferred.

"Why?"

"Why what?"

"Why are you doing this? Your family is convinced I'm a runaway, up to no good."

Reilly shook his head. "Not any more. I managed to get a quick call in to my Dad. They've handed Adam back his money, told him they were not going to take him on a client. I didn't know that. They did that the same day he came to them. Dad said his story didn't ring true and when they checked, they found out about the charges and his court date. Which is coming up very shortly."

She nodded. "I know. I have to be there." She shuddered in fear. "I'm so afraid, Reilly. He'll try everything he can to keep me from testifying." She tucked her hair behind her ear and Reilly drew a deep breath at the scar he saw behind her ear. "I mean, they can convict him with the evidence they have, but they said if I testify then it will make sure he is convicted and put away."

Reilly drew a deep breath, his eyes on the scar, his fingers itching to gently touch it. "That scar? It's from him?"

She looked up startled, her hand going to cover the scar before she pulled her hair forward. His hand stopped hers as he reached to tuck the hair back.

"Don't hide it from me, Aideen. It's okay. I've seen a lot worse." His eyes grew shadowed. "You have no ideas the wounds and scars I've seen over the last few years." He blinked, coming back to the present, and then pointed to her sandwich. "Eat. If you like, we can get out and walk along the shore for a bit when you're finished."

She looked at the sandwich, through the windshield at the water, and then at him. "Did anyone ever tell you that you are a very bossy man, Stuart?"

Reilly stared at her as with a smirk on her face, she raised the sandwich and bit into it before he shouted with laughter.

"Aideen, you are good for my soul. I needed that. My sisters always tell me that."

24

Chapter 4

As they walked the shore, their feet sinking into the sand, Aideen tucked her hair behind her ear before shoving her hands into her pockets and shivered. The wind was cold, she thought. Her grandmother would have said it was a wind that went right through a person. She kept stealing glances at her companion, wondering what his thoughts were. He was careful to keep a clear face, no emotions showing on it.

"Tell me about your family." When he looked over at him, she repeated herself. "Your family. Tell me about them."

"What would you like to know?"

She shrugged. "Forget I asked. I'm wasn't prying, just trying to get to know you."

Reilly sighed, his hand coming out to stop her. "It's okay, Aideen. I'm just not sure what you want to know." He reached for one of her hands and with it tight in his, walked them back to the truck, helping her inside and then reaching behind the seat for a blanket that he tucked over her.

Seating himself, he shifted so he was leaning against the door, one arm draped over the steering wheel, his eyes staring out the windshield and he began to talk. He realized she wasn't prying as she said but his eyes narrowed as he thought through her question. It wasn't idle curiosity he knew. He had learned quickly to read people, going into dangerous situations and countries to retrieve people as his father put it. Bringing them to safety, to their embassies in the countries, wasn't an easy task. It was one fraught with danger. He thought of the last retrieval his older brother had been on and how it had taken so much from him. He had decided then that he would not go overseas any more. He would talk with his father and find something else to do, whether with the company or on his own. He hadn't had a chance to do that, this situation with Aideen coming up so quickly.

He looked at her, finding her watching him, a closed look on her face, but he could see the worry and stress and downright terror in her eyes. He sighed. Lord, why me? Why put me here? You know I'm not good with the ladies who cry.

"I have two brothers and two sisters. Rory and his wife, Leah, just married. She actually has a bed and breakfast not far from here. We should head there. Redmond is overseas right now, he and Ryanne. This time at a conference. Regan is in the office, working. She and Rory were emotionally and mentally beat up a few months ago. We get along great. Dad and Mom made sure of that. We quarrel and have our differences, sometimes discussed in loud voices, but if you need one of them, they're right there." He paused, a look crossing his face she couldn't read. "I'm sorry, Aideen. I'm sorry you don't have that with your brother."

She nodded. "Thank you, Reilly. Not many people have said that over the years. It's usually condemning me for not getting along with him."

"Again, I'm sorry, Aideen." He twisted in his seat, reaching to start the truck. "We'll have some heat soon. Any idea where you want to head?"

"The nearest bus station is good. If I head to a large city, I can get lost there." She didn't look at him, staring instead out the window at the passing scenery.

"Not happening, Aideen. I'm not letting you wander around on your own. It's not safe."

She glared at him. "And where have you been for the last few weeks? Tell me that. I've had to learn to survive."

"You did, I agree with that. But things have changed. They found you. Do you really think you can hide in a big city? There are more people they can buy off to turn you it." He shot a hard look at her, seeing her face paling and fear flickering across it. "Didn't think of that, now did you? With me, at least you have a chance. If anything, Dad has places he can stick us away until the trial is over."

"I can't let you do that." She fumed, and he grinned to himself, thinking she was so like Ryanne. "Pull over. I said, pull over, Stuart. I want out."

He checked his rearview mirror, a frown on his face. "I don't think so. Duck down as much as you can, please? Hide your hair under your hat again, and pull that blanket up around your face. Like you're sleeping." When she didn't move, just stared at him, he barked. "Now. Do what I asked."

Aideen jumped at the harshness in his voice and quickly complied with his request. He could hear her muttering away, something about bossy men and that she would do just as well on her own and grinned, the levity needed at that moment.

He watched as the luxury car with the heavily tinted windows breezed past him, definitely going over the speed limit. His eyes narrowed. He pulled off onto a side road and headed in the opposite direction than they had been headed.

Pulling to the side of the road, he grabbed his phone and dialled. "Dad?"

"Reilly? Son, where are you? I'm at your place. It's been vandalized." He could hear the worry in his father's voice.

"Dad? Vandalized? When?" He shot a look at Aideen, finding her watching him, her eyes huge.

"Last night or early this morning. The police are going through your place right now. I can't tell if anything missing or not, though."

"Check the bottom file drawer. You'll find a list there of electronics and serial numbers and also photos of them. I have no work files there. Only personal ones and those don't have any information other than utilities and some correspondence with missions."

"All right. I talk to the officer for you. Where are you?"

"I was heading for Rory and Leah's, but turned around. Can you check out this plate?" Reilly rattled it off, his eyes on Aideen as she drew in her breath. "Just a sec, Dad." He pulled the phone from his mouth and stared at her. "Aideen? Do you know that vehicle?"

She nodded, terror on her face. "It's Adam's. Lord, help me. He's found me. I'm as good as dead now."

He could hear his father's voice, asking him who he was with and what was being said.

"Just a sec, Dad." He muted the phone and reached for her hand, finding hers ice cold. "Aideen, how did he find you?" He dropped the phone and reached for her back pack, handing it to her and dumping the food out of the bag behind the seat. "Here, stuff what clothing and whatnot you have in this." He watched and then taking the backpack, tossed it through a window, and pulled away. He picked up the phone again. "Dad, I'm driving. This will be short. I have Aideen Dennis with me. That's her brother's car. They've found her."

"Dear Lord, no!" He could hear the worry and anger in his father's voice. "I've been trying to find you for the last four weeks. We found that out and wanted to warn you. He's put a hit out on her. I'm sending someone to Rory. Stay with Aideen. Are you okay for cash?"

"For now, but I don't want to use my bank or credit card. Send Regan with some money to the old farmhouse. We'll head that way. After I check out my truck."

"Find another vehicle, Reilly. Chances are they've found yours."

"I will, Dad. This number is to a pay-as-you-go phone. No one should have it."

"Got it. Stay safe, son. You both are in our prayers."

"Thanks, Dad. Tell Regan to watch herself. I have no idea what these men are capable of."

"That I will. Call me when you can."

Reilly clicked off his phone, tossing it into a cup holder, and then searching for the road he wanted.

"Where are we heading now, Stuart? Obviously, you are not taking me to the big city."

"No. I am heading to our family farmhouse. No one knows we have it. It's in a friend's name."

"And you don't think they won't find it? They likely already have."

"I doubt that. Considering that it's a judge that is doing this for us, not likely."

She stared at him for a moment, before turning to the side window, muttering under her breath once more.

Reilly grinned as he drove towards safety, as he hoped and prayed. She was feisty, this Aideen, he thought.

Chapter 5

Aimlessly driving around, Reilly kept an eye out for the vehicle Aiceen had said was her brother. He was waiting for dusk to fall before heading into the farmhouse, just to be safe. He knew she was getting restless and finally pulled into a fast-food restaurant.

"I'm hungry. What do you want?" He sighed as she refused to respond. "Aideen, this is getting really old. What do you want?"

"I don't eat fast food." She finally looked at him and then past him at the vehicles in the lot.

"I'm sure they have salads. And milk or water or juice." He grinned as she brought her eyes back to him, mouth open to respond before she snapped it shut.

"Stuart, you are pushing it, do you know?" She crossed her arms and leaned her head against the window, fatigue weighing her very motions. "A salad and orange juice is fine." She dug into her pocket, pulling out some bills and thrust them at her.

He folded his hand over hers. "No, keep it. You'll need it for something." He stared at her for a moment before she moved restlessly. "I apologize. I shouldn't be staring. I went to say to buy something to make you beautiful, but you already are. Nothing you buy would make you any more beautiful."

She snorted at that. "Get real, Stuart. I'm not beautiful." She looked around. "So, are you buying or not?"

He shook his head. Someone has really done a number on her, haven't they, Lord? He pulled up, placed their orders and then when he had them, drove away, searching for somewhere they could get out and eat. He pulled into a picnic area, came around and helped her down. She glared at him again and once more he had to smother his grin. Feisty, isn't she, he thought. Just like Leah was. He stopped in his tracks and began to shake his head. No way, Lord. Not happening.

Aideen spun and stomped back, snatching the bags of food and heading for a table. Plopping the bags down, she sat, her eyes narrowed as she watched him just standing there. Shaking her head, she sighed.

"Stuart? Come on. Your burger will be cold if you don't stop woolgathering."

He looked up at that and started to laugh as he slid to a seat across from her. "Woolgathering? Now where did you ever get that word?"

She smirked. "I read. A lot. When I was a child, it's the only way I could escape." Sadness settled on her face for a moment before she shook it off.

He reached for her hand, tightening his grip when she tried to pull back. "I just want to pray over our food. That's all, Aideen." He watched as she visibly tried to relax herself. "Who made the pass at you?"

She looked up, startled at his words, before she paled. "How did you know?"

He shrugged. "I've see reactions like yours before. Too many times." He shook off his memories and reached for his food.

She ate, not tasting what she was eating before she stacked her garbage back into the bag, her eyes watching a little chipmunk scurrying around, its cheeks bulging with food. She listened to the sounds of the birds and insects and the faint lapping of the lake. She felt at peace, at least for a moment, before her memory turned back once more.

Aideen shook her head. No, she thought, the past stays where it belongs. In the past. All this stuff with Adam has me doubting the steps I have taken and that's not fair nor right. She jumped as she felt Reilly's hand on hers once more. She looked at him, but his attention was directed towards the road. He suddenly was on his feet, pulling her with him back into the trees. Not again, she thought. How did they find us?

The couple watched as a car pulled in, circled Reilly's truck slowly, and then pulled out. He listened and heard it stop just down the road from the entrance. He groaned. They couldn't go that way now. He waited and then heard the car moving off.

He pulled her with him on a run, shoving her into the truck, and sliding behind the wheel, keying the motor to life and taking off. Thankfully he didn't have traffic to contend with as he pulled out. He saw the man running after him and groaned again. They had been found, but how.

He tossed his phone at her. "Dial number one. That's my Dad."

"What?" She caught the phone and then stared at it before looking up at him. "Your Dad?"

"Yeah. Number one. Please, Aideen? This is no joke." He looked into the mirror and saw a vehicle coming up behind them. "Please, Aideen? And put it on speaker."

"Reilly?" He heard his Dad's voice. "You're driving. What is going on?"

"Someone found me. I'm trying to get away but I'm not sure I can. Does Dan still have the old truck at his place?"

"He does. He's been working on it. Head there. Where are you right now?"

Reilly could hear the rustle of paper as his father wrote down the location. "Now what, Dad? I've been driving in circles all day, waiting for night before I headed to the farmhouse."

"That's been compromised. I have no idea how. Redmond and Ryanne are back. He's looking into it. I can tell you, though, he's fuming and ready to fire any one of our staff who let it out."

"Tell him to wait. I think Aideen's brother has sources of information we don't know about. You can take it to the bank that they've researched all of us."

"I'm sure they have. Now, head for Dan's place. Ditch your truck somewhere and I'll have it towed home. Stay safe, son."

Reilly heard the click as his father hung up and watched from the corner of his eye as Aideen stuck the phone back into the cup holder. He was afraid, afraid that he couldn't protect her, afraid that someone would find her.

"Reilly, now what?" She hated the sound of fear in her voice.

He shrugged, his attention on the road and watching for the vehicle. He spun his wheel and took off on a side road and then repeated the maneuver multiple times before he finally spoke.

"Right now, I'm heading back into the town we just left. I'm ditching my truck. One of our workers has a truck I can use at his house. It will mean we'll need to take off on foot." He pulled into a parking lot and turned to her. "What do you have that you really need to take with you?"

She stared at him for a moment before she stuttered. "Just my Bible. I can replace everything." She snapped at him in a grumpy manner. "That is, if you let me, Stuart."

He grinned at her for a moment, then searched his phone before handing it to her. "Here. This is my sister, Regan. Let her know by text what sizes you wear and who you are and what you like to wear and colours as well. She loves to shop and finds bargains like no one else I know."

She stared at him for a moment, before she took the phone, hesitating for a moment before she began to type.

Chapter 6

Aideen stood in the shadows and watched as Reilly slipped through the dark to a decrepit shed at the back of a property. She just shook her head. How did he expect to find anything there and if he did, to get it out. She turned and listened, trying to hear if there were any footsteps. Reilly had parked in a shopping centre parking lot, locked the truck and walked away, her hand tight in his. He had not let her take anything with her, not even the Bible she so desperately needed with her. He had simply told her that someone would get it to her, that it needed to be examined. Examined for just what, she wondered.

She looked towards the building once more, hearing a motor coming her way. Her mouth dropped open at the truck he was driving. She shook her head. There is no way that decrepit vehicle that matched the shed it had come from out get them anywhere. She pulled the door open as Reilly stopped, surprised as how easily and quietly it opened.

She fastened her seatbelt, her mouth open to ask a question when Reilly shook his head, handing her a cap.

"Put that on and tuck your hair up under it. It might help conceal your identity." He had a cap on as well.

Pulling away from the house, Reilly's heart was in his mouth. He had no guarantees this would work, but his father seemed to think it would. His father's instincts were usually right on.

An hour later, he paused at the side of the road, watching for traffic. Seeing none, he pulled off onto a side road, driving for miles it seemed to Aideen afterwards, before he turned off into a little used lane, the overgrown trees and undergrowth brushing at the sides of the truck. He could tell someone had been along there that afternoon. Please, Lord, let it be Regan or Dad. Not someone we'll have to flee from again. He shot a quick look at Aideen. She rested her head on the back of the seat, her eyes closed. He wasn't sure if she was sleeping or not but he knew she was at her limit. In fact, he didn't have much more to give himself.

He paused before he entered the clearing, the truck motor running quietly as he searched the area. His eyes narrowed as he stared at the car sitting near the barn and nodded. Good, he thought. Regan made it. Now to get Aideen in.

He parked near Regan's car and turned off the motor, taking time to thank God for His protection that day and turned to study Aideen. She had not stirred.

He sighed. There seemed to be no easy way to do this, he thought. He slipped from his seat and around the truck, opening her door, and then reaching to undo the seatbelt. As he gathered her into his arms, he heard the faint sigh and felt her turn her face into his shoulder. A murmured thank you came from her.

Reilly stood for a moment, his eyes on her face, emotions running through him that he had never felt before. He didn't date much, didn't want a lady thinking she was his choice for life. His work kept him busy, he was overseas a lot, and just had not had the time to find his lady. Lord, I have no idea what's going on right now, but You do. Guard our hearts. She's someone I could come to care for and that's not right. Not when she's in such danger. She doesn't need that extra burden.

He walked slowly towards the house, his thoughts racing as to what they would face. He knew now what Rory had meant, about being caught in the eye of a storm. He felt like he was caught on the edge of a huge storm, unable to break free, and having no safety net to catch him.

Regan stood for a moment on the porch, watching her brother walk up the steps, and then opening the door, pointed towards one of the bedrooms, frowning as he shook his head and headed for the living room instead. He carefully laid his burden on the couch and took the blanket Regan held out for him, tucking it around Aideen, pausing to brush the hair back from her face. He turned, pointing to the kitchen.

"That's a fresh pot of coffee, Reilly. I have food here for you both. Dad said to have it ready but he wasn't sure when or even if you would make it."

Reilly paused for a moment before he wrapped his sister in his arms. "Thanks, Regan. I can eat. I'm starved in fact. Aideen needs sleep more than food right now. She's at her limit, I would say." He reached for the coffee pot, pouring them both a cup, before he turned to the stove, inhaling the aroma of the stew Regan had ready before ladling out a bowl for himself. He held the ladle up for Regan and she shook her head.

"I ate a while ago. I wasn't sure when you'd pull in." She reached for the biscuits she had left in the oven. "I left them in the oven as it cooled, hoping to keep them warm a bit."

Reilly dropped a kiss on his sister's cheek. "Thanks, sis. Of all the meals you could have made, your stew is just what I need." He ate, his gaze drifting every few minutes to the living room doorway.

"Reilly?" Regan waited until he looked at her. "What's her story? Dad didn't say much today, other than that the two of you are on the run."

"Her brother has a hit out on her." He looked up at Regan as she gasped. "That's right. He wants her dead. She turned him in, I'm still not clear why. She doesn't say much."

Regan stared at him, then rose, heading for the living room, returning with a stack of files. "Dad sent this. He wants you to go over them." She sighed. "She really is in trouble, isn't she?"

"She is. And I don't know how long I can keep her safe. We shouldn't be travelling around like we are, as a couple. That's not the way we work."

Regan nodded. "I know. Dad wants me to stay with you two, for now anyway."

Reilly studied his sister for a moment. "And how do you feel about that?"

She tucked a strand of hair behind her ear, her eyes on the folders. "I don't know, Reilly, to tell you the truth. Let's look through what Dad sent." She paused, her eyes on her brother. "I have my laptop, but I don't want to power it up if I can help it. Dad thinks we've been compromised and he has Redmond and Ryanne looking into that."

"Not Peter?" When she shook her head, he sat back in his chair. "Dad's really concerned then, isn't he? Peter's the best at finding that kind of stuff."

"He is."

Aideen roused slowly, her eyes flickering open, and she felt a moment of panic, not knowing where she was. She sat up quickly, searching for Reilly, relaxing once she heard his voice. She rose, heading for the kitchen, stopping in the doorway as she saw he wasn't alone.

Regan stopped her hand as she was reaching for another file, her eyes on the door. Reilly spun and then rose, walking over to Aideen, stopping in front of her, ducking his head to study her face before he nodded.

"Hungry? Regan has some stew hot for you. And there's juice in the fridge." He took her hand when she didn't move, leading her to a seat at the table. "Aideen, this is my sister, Regan. She's to stay with us for now. Another set of eyes is always helpful." He dished up her plate and set it and a bottle of juice in front of her. Resuming his seat, he watched as she stared first at Regan and then at him. "Aideen? What are you thinking?"

"Stuart, you just don't give up, do you?"

Regan shot her brother a look at how he was addressed, seeing him just grin.

"Nope. Not when it means keeping you alive. That's our aim. Regan and I make a great team, and we've just elected you to it. So live with it." He pointed to her plate. "Eat."

"I'm not a dog. Don't order me to eat." She glared at him, not catching the smile Regan hid.

"Did I say you were? Miss Dennis, would you do me the honour of eating the meal set before you, prepared by loving hands? It is delicious, if you must know." Reilly's attention was back on the folder he had opened, missing the look on Aideen's face. He heard a faint chuckle from Regan and looked up at her, seeing the mirth in her eyes. "And no comments from the peanut gallery."

"Reilly! Don't treat your sister that way!" Aideen was shocked at his words.

"It's okay, Aideen. Really it is. I know he loves me. This is his way of showing it. We talk like this all the time. No offence is given and none is taken. You learn that fast in our family." Regan pointed to her plate. "Please, eat. If you don't want that, I can find something else for you."

"No, this is fine." Aideen spooned a mouthful of stew into her mouth and paused, her eyes closing. "This is so good. I have never tasted anything like this."

Finally shoving aside her plate, Aideen studied Reilly, seeing the frown and the dark look on his face.

"Reilly?" When he looked up at her soft question of his name, she shook her head. "What have you found? You re frowning."

He sighed, his eyes on her face. "I don't like what I'm reading. If you will, let me go through it all, and then I need to talk to you. Regan, I know you're writing down your own questions. This will likely take all night. Did Dad say when he wanted us to come in?"

"He doesn't. Not yet. He's not sure Aideen would be safe at one of the houses in town. He's lining up a number for us to use and also different vehicles that we can switch to."

Aideen stared at them. "He can't do that. That's too much trouble."

Reilly reached for her hand, his grasp tight but gentle, she thought. "Trust me, Aideen. This is nothing compared to what we usually have to do." He shook his head at her. "I guess I haven't really explained what we do. We are asked to go in and do what they call extractions. We go in and bring people out of places, some very dangerous places, and bring them home or to their country's embassy. It is dangerous work."

Aideen watched closely before she shook her head. "I don't get it. Why?"

"Why what?"   Reilly shared a look with Regan.

"Why did you decide to try and find me? What's in it for you?   If, as you say, your father turned him down, who's paying you?"   She was becoming upset.

Reilly reached for her hands, his thumbs rubbing along the back of hers. "No one is, but that's okay, Aideen.   Really, it is.   Every once in a while, we get asked to find someone and the person asking can't pay us.   The person we've been asked to find is more important than the money."

She stared at him, not sure if he was speaking the truth.

Regan had been watching closely. "He's right, Aideen. We do that. Dad always has."

Aideen shook her head. "But why me? I'm sure you turn down lots of work."

"We do."   Reilly and Regan shared a look. "Dad is the one who evaluates every request that comes through. He decided that we needed to find you, bring you in, and get your side of the story." Reilly saw Regan nodding. "We've gone overseas to do just that. This time, you in our home province. That hasn't made it any easier. You know how to hide and hide well."

Aideen snorted.   "Well, yeah, I guess I do. He's been after me for years. And not just for this." She paused, her head going down.   The siblings shared a look before Reilly noticed the tears dropping.

"Aideen? Talk to us?" When she shook her head, he shifted his chair closer to her and wrapped an arm around her. "What did he do to you? What did he threaten you with?"

She looked up, and both siblings drew in a sharp breath. "Reilly, he's brutal. He's killed my cats, my dog. One of my little kittens right in front of me when I was just young. He told me he would do the same to me. I was so afraid. I remember talking to Mom one time and she just looked at me, told me to grow up, that Adam would never do anything like that. She had asked him and he denied it. Said I had done it."

Reilly drew her into a hug and felt the tears soaking into his shirt. Regan rose, bringing back a warm damp cloth she handed to her brother.

Aideen finally moved away from Reilly, his arms dropping away. She took the cloth handed her and swiped at her face, not looking at either Reilly or Regan.

Regan shot Reilly a swift look and when he shook his head, she rose and came around to Aideen.

"Aideen, I am sure you could just some time to get cleaned up. Come on. I'll show you were the shower is and you can take a look at the clothes I brought. Hopefully, I've done well and there's something there you can wear."

Reilly watched the two woman walk away and then reached for his phone, turning it over and over in his hand before he finally dialled his father's number.

"Reilly? You're safe?" He could hear the relief in his father's voice.

"For now, but I'm not sure for how long. Regan said you're setting up a network of houses and vehicles?"

"That was the plan, but he's found out where you are and is systematically searching for you in the area. We need you out of there. I'm sorry, son. It means moving tonight."

Reilly turned to look behind him as he heard Regan's footsteps. "I get that, Dad. We've been working through the material, but Aideen seems to think there's more to it than just what she's said."

"There is. I need you to come home and now."

"Okay. I'll send Regan on ahead then."

"No, stay together. Leave her car where it is. The vehicle you're using? Head to the Brown's. Leave your vehicle on the street and head for the downtown area. I'll text the details of what you're looking for." He was gone before Reilly could question him further.

"Reilly? What did Dad say?"

"We need to leave. How long will Aideen be?"

"She said ten minutes. I'm sure it will be less. Why?"

"We have to move and move now. Pack up what we need. Anything we can't fit into a backpack stays." He was swiftly stuffing folders into his backpack and then rising, looked around for anything they had missed. "Tidy up as best you can. I'm heading out to look around."

"Reilly! What did Dad say? I know you called him."

"He didn't say much other than he wanted us home and for us to stay together." He looked at his sister, not sure how to proceed. "I don't like this, Regan. Something's happened for Dad to be like this." He paced, a hand rubbing at his face. "I'm not sure that we should stay together."

"We should, if Dad feels that strongly about it." She paused as she heard Aideen's steps on the hallway. "You get to explain it to your lady."

Reilly stared at Regan for a moment, opened his mouth to deny that, then clamped it close as Aideen entered the kitchen, her eyes shifting between the two.

"What happened?" When neither answered, she spun and stomped towards Reilly. "Stuart? Are you hiding something from? You had better not be. If you are, I'm out of here." She waited and then headed for the door.

Reilly's hand came out and stopped her. "Aideen. Enough! We're needing to leave. Now."

She stopped and her eyes slid closed. "He's found me again, hasn't he? When will it stop?" She turned abruptly, her hands up to shove Reilly away from her. "It will only stop when I'm dead. And he'll kill anyone who's with me. So, leave, will you? And take your sister with you." Tears hovered just below the surface and she tried to suppress them.

Reilly gave an inaudible sound and then swept her into a tight hug, his head against her. "Aideen, we will not leave you. We will do everything we can to keep you safe. Trust us on that."

Regan watched for a moment, then moved around, gathering up what she could. Clothes and personal items she stuffed into a backpack, quenched the fire in the fireplace, and then headed for the kitchen, making sure it was tidy. She finally turned to Reilly, keys held up.

"Reilly, we need to move. I have a bad feeling we're out of time."

"I pray not, Regan. Aideen, here. Your coat." He shrugged into his, watched as Regan turned off lights, and then with Aideen's hand tight in his, headed for the cars, stopping as he heard a sound, and then pointed towards the barn. The three ran for it, sliding inside.

Reilly shut the door and then stood, listening. He sighed. There would be no way they could get to the cars. How were they to reach town? He searched for his phone, pulling it out and muting it. He didn't want it ringing and alerting anyone to where they were.

He looked around and nodded as Regan pointed towards a back door. Aideen's hand in his, he tugged her through the barn and then out the back door, his eyes watchful. He knew Regan was watching as well, coming behind them. They ran for the cornfield behind the barn, finding a path through the growing stalks until they reached the other side. He paused them then, giving them a chance to catch their breath.

"Now what, Reilly? I got a quick text off to Dad, then shut my phone down."

"Thanks, sis. Now we just have to find a place to hole up for a bit. There are caves down here, aren't there?"

"Not any more. I heard they destroyed them after those kids got hurt in one."

Reilly blew out a breath. "That's not good. Where can we go then?"

"There's that old shack about two miles from here. You can't find it unless you know where it is."

"Lead the way, Regan." He turned to watch Aideen for a moment. "Aideen, are you up to this?"

She snorted. "It doesn't look as if I have much choice, now does it?" She pulled at her hand and frowned at him when he didn't release it.

Chapter 7

Coming to a halt, Reilly motioned for the two woman to wait where they were as he moved towards the old shack, his eyes searching in the brightening dawn light for signs of any traffic or footprints. He saw none but he knew that didn't mean a whole lot. He moved around the cabin in narrowing circles. He finally stood in front of the door, reached to touch it, pausing as it swung open in front of him. He didn't have a good feeling and turned and ran for the woods, away from where Regan and Aideen were standing. The sound of a blast broke through the morning air, startling the birds and animals into silence and sudden flight. He hit the ground behind a tree and edged around so he could look at the cabin. It was totally destroyed, the pile of debris shocking him. He laid his head down. Thank you, Lord. I heard that voice of Yours and stopped.

He rose, making his way carefully back to the two woman. Regan turned a grim face to him and shook her head, pointing back the way he had come. He stood for a moment before he nodded and then reached to pull Aideen to her feet. The shocked look on her face broke his heart and he just swept her into a hug before he caught her hand and pulled her with him, following Regan.

When he felt they were far enough away, he paused, Regan stopping beside him.

"How did they know, Reilly?"

He shrugged. "I think they've been searching around us. I still think they are tracking us somehow." He sighed. "We have a couple of miles to go but check your shoes, Regan."

He sat Aideen down on a rock and knelt, pulling off her shoes and feeling along them, a grim look on his face as his hand paused. He reached for his pocket knife, slitting the sole carefully and then pulling back his hand, opening it to show Regan what he held.

"GPS?" At his nod, she drew a sharp breath. "They've known where she was the whole time?"

"I would hazard a guess that they have. Unless she's been wearing other shoes. Aideen?"

Aideen shook herself and looked up. "I had another pair I usually wore but they were destroyed in the fire. Those are just new ones I bought a week or so ago. How did that get in there?" She pointed at the tracker. "And who?"

"Somehow I don't think it was your brother. Whoever is after him has found you first and has been using you to try and find him." Reilly stood, pitching the GPS away from them.

"Was that such a good idea, Reilly? We might need that for evidence." Regan's dry voice broke through the silence.

"Yes, it was. If we keep it, they keep tracking us.   Now, Aideen, anything else that might have something in it?"

She shook her head.   "No, I don't have anything left from the cabin." She leaned forward, her face pale. "Is that what they did the day I bought them and they took the shoes to the back for a moment? I couldn't figure that out."

"I would suspect that. They likely narrowed in to where they thought you were, put out word that they wanted contacted if you were seen. Most people would have refused, but if there was enough money involved, others would jump at the chance."

Regan pointed towards the road. "We can't go that way. They are likely patrolling the roads, looking for us." She reached for her backpack, setting in on the ground and digging through it. "Here. I packed some water and sandwiches." She passed them to the other two. "Eat, Aideen. You'll be glad you did. One thing we have learned over the years is to take time to eat when there's an opportunity. You never know when you'll get another one."

"Aideen?" Reilly waited until she looked up at him. His heart broke for the devastation he saw there. He crouched back down beside her, reaching for her hand, and clasping it tight as he prayed for her.

Aideen stared at the head bowed over her hand and wondered at the peace she was beginning to feel, the safety, the security, the peace she had not felt in all her life, she realized. What was it about him? She looked up to find Regan watching her, a smile on her face. She then looked up at the sky.

Lord, I know You are there. Please keep my friends safe. I don't care about me. Just bring them through this and back to their family, unharmed.

Reilly stood and moved away from the women, studying the terrain around him, assessing the best way to move. He had never had to go on the run in his home province. He was unsure where to head. He turned back to study the two woman, knowing Aideen would set the pace. He had no idea how she would manage, she was that tired. Regan, he had no doubts that she would keep up with him.

"Reilly?" Regan moved towards him, backpack in place, Aideen right behind her. "We're near that new trail that's been put in. Can we use ii?"

He nodded. "For a bit. It takes us into town. How far do you figure?"

"Five kilometres, I would say."

He nodded. "I think you're right. Let's go. Regan, you're in front for now. Aideen, please stay between us."

Aideen glared at him as she moved past him. "Stuart, you're pushing again. I can keep up with you. You'll be the one lagging behind."

He grinned at her feistiness and prayed that she was right, that she would be able to keep up with them. Stopping finally at the edge of town, he pointed towards the park benches and then led them that way.

"Aideen? You okay?" He grinned at she frowned at him and then sighed.

"I am, Reilly. Now what? Where do we go?"

"I'm working on that." He pulled out his phone as he felt the vibrations. He had been ignoring it. He glanced at him and his face became grim. He motioned to Regan and handed over his phone, hearing her quick gasp of disbelief before her eyes lit on Aideen and then rose to him, a question in them.

"Stuart, what are you hiding from me?"

Reilly gave her a quick grin. "You really do need to decide what name you're calling me, you know?" He sat beside her, an arm around her.

"Your arm?"

"Hush, Aideen. We need to talk." He paused, taking a deep breath, before he continued. "That text message was from my Dad. I have news." He paused again, not quite sure how to proceed.

"Spit it out, then   This suspense isn't doing either one of us any good."

He shook his head at her.   "It's bad news, Aideen.   It's your brother.   He's been found dead, along with the two men he had working for him. When the authorities went to advise your parents, they found them dead as well."   His arm tightened as he felt her body stiffen and then relax against him.

"It's over?   I can go home?"   He hated to destroy the hope he heard in her voice.

"Not yet.   Dad said they don't know who did this.   The police have asked him to continue to provide protection for you, until they can do some more investigating."

"It's not over.   Reilly, what am I do to?   I can't continue to run, not putting you at risk."   She turned to stare at him, a frown coming over her face at the look on his.   "Reilly?"

He shook his head.   "I'm thinking through something."   He looked up at his sister.   "Regan, how far to Niagara Falls?"

She spun, her mouth dropping open before she snapped it closed, and shook her head at him, eyes narrowing.   "Not that. Reilly."

He shrugged, his eyes on Aideen, seeing her trying to process what he had told her.   "I can't continue to run around the country like this."   He rose, pulling Aideen to her feet, keeping her hand tight in his.   "Let's find our vehicles, Regan.   Dad said there were two.   We need to split up again. They'll be looking for the three of us."

"Dad said Redmond was here."

"I know.   Go home with him, Regan.   Please?"

She finally nodded, walking away from her brother. She prayed, harder than she had since Rory had his trouble a few months previously. She knew Reilly had a plan, a plan he wasn't willing to share with them, and she also knew that whatever it was, he would have prayed hard about it.

Aideen watched Regan walk away, suddenly feeling lost. She turned to Reilly, finding him watching her.

"Reilly, what is your plan?"

He sighed. "I need to talk to you about something. I've prayed about it but I still not sure if it's the way to go." He walked in the direction Regan had taken, finally stopping by a truck. He felt along the bottom of it, finding a key, then unlocking the door and helping Aideen in. He walked around, his steps slow, fatigue suddenly weighing him down. It was only eight in the morning but felt a lot later. He slid behind the wheel, inserting the key into the ignition, and then just sitting there.

"Reilly?" Aideen's voice was quiet, barely audible. "What are you plotting now?"

He twisted in his seat, a prayer rising within him. Lord, am I doing what I should? If we don't, then I can't continue to provide care for her. It just wouldn't be right.

"Aideen, I have no idea what your life has been like, other than for the last couple of months I have been tracking you. You are a beautiful, talented lady, and I see your love and trust in God coming through. I have a suggestion to make, something that I need you to think about and unfortunately given that we need to stay together, I can't do that as we are. I won't destroy your reputation. That's too important for you."

"What are you suggesting, Reilly?" She thought through what he was saying. "Reilly? No, we can't."

"Just listen for a moment, and then think about. I suggest we get married, a marriage in name only, just until you're safe and the ones after you are caught. Then we have it annulled and you're free to move on." He watched as she began to shake her head and saw the moment she understood what he was offering.

"You would do that, Reilly? You would marry me and then let me go?" Her voice was a whisper, uncertain in tone, but held a sense of wonder at his offer.

"I would, Aideen. I would offer you my protection as your husband. It would make it easier to protect you. I haven't talked to my family, but that doesn't matter. What matters is keeping a beautiful lady who I've come to care about as a friend safe." He started the truck and pulled away, stopping as her hand was laid on his arm.

"I don't get it, Reilly. Most people in your position wouldn't care less. And I can't imagine you offering this to everyone."

He shook his head, a shadow crossing his face. "You're correct, Aideen. I have never done this before. In fact, I haven't been dating. Work has been that crazy. Besides I don't want someone I'm dating to think I'm there for the long haul, that marriage is on the table, when I just want to spend time with a friend." He looked over at her. "You're important to me, Aideen. I can honestly say I haven't felt like this before."

She nodded, folding her hands together, and then staring out the window. "How long do I have to make a decision?"

"Not long, unfortunately. I would like to do it today, if you agree." Her eyes shots to him as her mouth opened and closed without any words. "We can get a license and get married today. I have a friend near Niagara Falls who's a minister. I'm sure he would be willing to perform the ceremony." He pulled away from the curb, heading for another town.

"That's a lot to ask, Reilly. I just don't know. How long before you reach this town?" She refused to look at him, keeping her eyes trained out the side window.

"About two hours. I'm sorry, Aideen. I wish I could come up with another plan to protect you and keep your reputation intact. If Regan had been able to stay with us, it would have been different." He watched closely to see if they had a tail and didn't see one.

Chapter 8

Aideen watched as, seated back in the truck, Reilly tucked the marriage license into a pocket of his jacket and then paused. He turned to her, ready to say something and paused.

"Reilly?" Her voice was soft and questioning. At this point, she was too tired and worn out to think properly. She had prayed about what he asked, had agreed to this step, but was waiting.

"This is so unfair to you, Aideen. Maybe we shouldn't do this." He watched as her eyes slid closed and a single tear tracked down her face. He reached to wipe it away, startling her with his gentle touch. "We don't have to do this."

"But you think it might be the only way?" Her eyes studied his, finding determination in his.

"It might well be the only way to keep you alive. All I know is that I can't keep running around the province, trying to protect you, on our own. It's not who I am or who you are."

She sighed. "I know." Her eyes strayed outside the window, studying the shops around her.

His eyes followed her line of sight and then he was out of the truck, pulling her out and then along with him, stopping in front of one of the shops. She shot him a startled look and began to shake her head as he pushed open the door and entered.

A saleswoman approached, a smile in place, as she studied the young couple.

"May I help you?"

"Yes, please." Reilly studied Aideen's face. "She needs a wedding dress, simple I think and not expensive. She doesn't like expensive clothes."

Aideen had turned to him as he spoke, her mind in a whirl, trying to determine how he had gotten to know her so well, before she followed the woman to the back.

Reilly paused for a moment, his eyes out the door before he was out of the store and into the men's store next door, returning shortly dressed in a navy blue suit and white shirt, a striped tie in place. He looked around, not seeing Aideen but hearing her voice.

Aideen stared at herself in the mirror in wonder. This couldn't be her, now could it? The saleswoman stepped back, knowing she had found the best gown for Aideen. Aideen turned, her eyes towards the curtain. She moved towards them, not hearing the soft words from the saleswoman. She needed to see Reilly and know that he approved of her gown.

Reilly turned from where he had stood, looking out of the window, and drew in a deep breath. She is truly beautiful, Lord, but doesn't know it. I wish it was my right to cherish her for the rest of our lives. Whatever had been left of his heart for Aideen to capture had been captured.

Aideen stood, uncertainty in place. "Reilly?"

He walked towards her, reaching for her hands. "Aideen, you are so beautiful." He ducked at bit to look into her eyes. "Are you sure now?"

She nodded. "I am. I need to change back into my own clothes first though. I can't wear this out of here." She studied him. "You've bought a suit."

"I did. It was only right." He watched as she walked away from him before he turned to another saleswoman, putting in a request. She nodded, and hurried to the back of the store, returning shortly with what he had requested.

He tucked her back into his truck and stood for a moment, not feeling any eyes on them for the moment, not feeling a sense of being watched or in danger. Good, he thought. Let us get through this, Lord. I'm still not sure, dear Lord, that this is the right step but I have not felt Your hand staying this. If it's not what you want, please stop us.

He drove away from the city, heading for the shore of Lake Erie again and to a small town, stopping in front of a small house and turning off the truck. He had sent a text message to his friend and had a response back, questioning his sanity. He had laughed at that and told his friend to wait until he met his lady. Unbeknownst to him, that was how he had begun to think of her. His lady.

Reilly turned to Aideen, catching the apprehension flickering across her face. He reached for her hand, praying for them.

Aideen started as she felt his hand and then listened to his words, relaxing as she did so.

A tap at his window had Reilly jumping before he turned and then opened his door, stepping out and closing the door behind him.

Richard Stevens studied his young friend for a moment before he pulled him into a hug. Richard was a good friend of the Stuart family, watching the five siblings grow up. He knew that Reilly was not making this decision lightly.

"Reilly? It's good to see you. How many months has it been?"

“Too many, Richard. Is Meg around?”

“She is. She thinks you’re crazy too, but wants to meet your lady.”

Reilly nodded. “Aideen. There’s a story there, but it’s better if you don’t know it. Not yet, anyway.”

Richard ducked to look through the window, finding Aideen watching him and then turning her eyes to Reilly. He sighed. Young love, and they don’t know they love each other. Not yet. “Bring your lady in, Reilly. And bring whatever it is you need to change into. Although I would say you’re ready now.”

Reilly laughed. “I am. It’s Aideen that will need to change.” He walked around to her door, opening it and watching her closely before holding out his hand.

Hand in hand they followed Richard into his house, his wife, Meg, waiting for them.

Four hours later, the couple walked away, Reilly tucking Aideen back into the truck, before he stood, staring around. No sense of danger tickled at him and he was glad. He stepped back to the porch for a final word with Richard and Meg and then ran for his truck, sliding inside and pulling away.

Aideen stared at him and then down at her hand. How did he have time to find the rings, Lord? I wasn’t that long trying on a dress but he managed to find a band that fits. But why an engagement ring? This is not a true marriage, just one to try and keep me safe.

“Reilly? Where are we heading?” Aideen turned to watch him.

“Home, I think. For now, any way.” He caught the uncertainty in her voice. “Don’t worry.

They will welcome you." He sighed as his phone rang and he pulled off to the side of the road and reached for it. "It's my Dad."

Her hand flew to her mouth. "Reilly, what will they think? I've put you in such danger." Her hands shook as she tried to clasp them together.

Reilly reached for her hands. "Hush, Aideen. They'll welcome you in. I suspect Regan has talked to Mom and Dad already."

He finally answered his phone. "Dad?"

"Heading home, son?" He heard an unspoken question in his father's voice.

"We are, Dad. Unless we need to run somewhere."

"I would suggest you do that. Find some place you can stop for the night. We have a situation here."

Reilly's face tightened. "I see. All right, Dad. That's what I'll do. I'll be in touch later."

"Do that, son. Put your phone on speaker for a moment, please."

Reilly did so, his eyes on Aideen's face as she frowned at him.

"Aideen? I know you're there. Reilly's Mom and I…We….We just want to welcome you to our family. Reilly will take care of you and bring you home to us as soon as he can." The connection was broken at that point.

Aideen stared at the phone, her mouth open, before she looked up at Reilly. "Did he really just say that? How did he know?"

"He did. Regan. I didn't tell her but she had an idea of what we were up to."

"Even knowing how dangerous I am to you, he says that? I don't get it."

Reilly sighed, knowing he could not explain it to her, not until she met his parents. "It's who they are, what they do. My oldest brother, Rory, had taken some personal time and found a bed and breakfast to stay at. Long story short, Leah, the owner, was facing some dangerous times. Mom and Dad ended up there and helped her. They knew Leah would become part of our family before Rory even spoke to her and welcomed her in." He paused, thinking back over that time. "I ended up kidnapped with Leah at one point."

"Reilly! Now you tell me." She stared at him. "Is that going to happen again?"

"I pray not, but only God knows what's ahead of us." He pulled back onto the road and headed towards the north of the area. "I need to find somewhere we can stay for tonight. Any ideas?"

She continued to stare at him before she spoke. "About three hours from here, there's a small motel. Out of the way, run down, but clean. You don't find it easily."

"Okay, then. Directions, please?"

She shook her head at him as she proceeded to give him the directions, wondering that he didn't need to write them down.

Chapter 9

Shutting the motel door behind him, Reilly turned to set the food he had purchased on the table, assessing Aideen as he did so. He sighed. No, she's not doing well. The stress of running and watching over her shoulder has caught up with her. He approached her, his hands on her shoulder.

"Aideen? Are you okay?"

She gave an abrupt nod. "I'm just tired, Reilly. Tired of running, of watching over my shoulder. When will it end?"

"I pray soon, my love." He drew her into a hug, his arms strong around her. "I'll take you to Mom tomorrow and see what she can do for you." He leaned back, studying her face. "Let's eat and then you can get some sleep."

"You need to sleep too. You're running on fumes right now, aren't you?"

He laughed. "Just about."

Reilly watched later as Aideen slept, her left hand tucked close to her mouth. He shook his head, still not sure if this had been the correct step to take, but knowing he had had to take it. His head bowed as he prayed, feeling the danger closing in on them and knowing in his own strength, he would not survive or be able to protect his lady.

He opened his eyes, staring at the mottled pattern of the carpet, and sighed. Yes, he thought, she's my lady. The one who has haunted my dreams for years. But I have to let her go when this is done and I'm not sure that I can. It's what You want, Lord.

So far, I have peace that I have taken the right step, but I have no idea what is ahead.

He finally rose, kicking off his boots and shoving aside the spread, laid down beside Aideen, pulling the spread back up on him. He needed to sleep and that was a given. He had to rest, knowing that tomorrow might bring danger and he needed to be alert.

Reilly stirred in the early morning hours, not sure what had awakened him. He moved and felt a weight on his shoulder and looked down. Aideen had turned to him in the night and he had caught her close to him, her head resting over his heart. He sighed. Lord, what am I to do? He gently moved her back to her pillow and rose, sitting for a moment on the edge of the bed to watch her sleep and then reached for his boots, heading outside to check the truck and the area around them. He frowned for a moment, feeling a presence approaching.

He spun and ran for the room, locking the door after him, and then rousing Aideen.

"Reilly? What is it?" She was instantly alert, sliding from under the covers, ready to run as she had slept fully dressed. She reached for her sneakers, sliding into them.

"They must be getting close to us. We need to move."

She nodded, handing him the backpacks and running for the truck. He tucked her in, dropping the backpacks behind the seat, and then running around the truck, firing it up, and taking off as silently as he could. He breathed a sigh of relief that they had managed to get away. He headed for home, eyes watchful, not seeing anything close.

Aideen watched as Reilly turned into a winding road, stopping at a wrought iron gate and keying in a passcode before the gates opened and he drove through. She turned her head to watch the gates closed, feeling safe for the first time in a while.

Reilly pulled to a stop in a circular driveway and turned off the ignition, his eyes on his childhood home before he turned to Aideen, watching as she studied the house before she,

"Not what you expected?" A grin lit up his face.

"No. I expected a mansion of some kind, not a simple farmhouse. You amaze me, Stuart."

"It was Dad's parents' home, where he grew up. We were raised here. There's love and warmth and caring in this home, Aideen. You're part of it now."

She snorted. "Just until this is over, isn't it?" She stopped speaking, biting at her lip, not answering when he spoke to her.

Reilly looked up to see his mother standing on the porch, a hand shading her eyes, as she waited for them to approach. He slid from the wheel and headed around the truck, opening the door and waiting for Aideen to take his hand. She finally let him help her from the truck, her movements stilling as she saw his mother waiting for them.

"She doesn't bite, Aideen. In fact, I think she'll just take you in as another daughter."

"How can she? Doesn't she know this is temporary?"

He nodded. ' She does. It doesn't matter to her. You're my wife and that's all that matters."

Naomi Stuart watched as her son stood with his new bride, waiting for them to walk towards them before she went down the steps, reaching to hug

Reilly and hold him tight for a moment before she turned to Aideen. Seeing the apprehension and uncertainty on her face, Naomi did what she did best. She simply enveloped the younger woman into a hug and held her tight for a few moments, a prayer audible only to the two of them on her lips. She finally stepped back, her hands on Aideen's upper arms and then nodded.

"Welcome, Aideen. We have been waiting for you for years." An arm around both her son and his bride, she turned them towards the house. "In with you now. I know you've been on the road already. Reilly, take your bride up to your suite. She'll want to clean up. Regan was by and left some clothes for her. Bring her to the kitchen when you're both cleaned up."

Reilly stood for a moment, watching as Aideen paced the room, stopping to touch his books and then standing at the window, staring out, before she turned to him.

"Why. Reilly? Why did she say that?"

He moved to stand in front of her, a puzzled frown on his face. "Say what? What did Mom say?"

"She welcomed me to the family, that they've been waiting for me for years? Doesn't she know this is temporary?"

Reilly sighed. Thanks, Mom, he thought. Now how do I explain this to her?

"She does, but she sometimes phrases things in a way that takes people back." He didn't continue and add that she was usually right. "I think she just wanted you to know you were welcome here."

She finally nodded, looking past him at the bed. "Who left the clothes?"

"Regan. She still has your list from the other day. The bathroom's through that door. Go on, take a shower or bath. Take as long as you like. There's no rush."

"But your Mom will be waiting on breakfast for us." She was beginning to feel panicked.

"No, she won't. She'll be ready when we are. That's how she is." He could see that she was still upset. "Go on, Aideen. Go ahead and clean up. I'm finding another room to do that and I'll be back." He watched as she finally nodded, sorted through the clothes on the bed, hesitating as she tried to decide what to take, and then disappeared through the bathroom door. He heard the water start running and turned to his dresser, knowing he had a few minutes. He headed for the guest bathroom, shutting the door and then staring at his face, seeing the stress and strain on it, the stubble that had grown over the last few days and groaned. Not the way he wanted to have his wedding yesterday, looking like a ruffian.

He finally walked back to his suite and stood just inside the door, listening for Aideen, hearing soft muttering through the closed door, and smiled. She is telling herself off, isn't she, Lord? How do I reach her? How do we keep her safe?

Aideen hesitated for a moment, her eyes on Reilly, before she walked towards him and into his hug. I could grow to like this, she thought.

"Ready, my love? Let's go see what Mom has for us."

She stared at him for a moment and then shook her head, taking his hand as he headed down the steps, stopping in the kitchen doorway for a moment. He looked down at her, finding her watching him.

"It's okay. They don't bite." She shook her head at him before he led her to the table and pulled back a chair for her. "Sit, Aideen. I'll find something for us for breakfast."

She hesitated and then slid onto the chair, her hands rubbing up and down her thighs. She heard footsteps behind her and froze.

"Reilly! You're here, son, and safe." Riordan pulled his son into a hug and held on just a bit longer than normal. "You're okay?" He stepped back to study Reilly before he looked around him. "And this is Aideen?"

Reilly nodded. "It is, Dad. This is Aideen Dennis Stuart."

Aideen drew in a deep breath at how she was introduced, not looking up. She heard Riordan stop beside her before a chair was pulled out and a hand reached for her.

"Aideen, it is a pleasure to welcome you to our home and to our family." He smiled kindly at her as her eyes shot up to his. "You're safe here. We'll have some discussions to have but know this. You are now a part of our family. Our house is your house. We'll let you have a few days to relax."

"That's the thing, Mr. Stuart. I'm not really a part of your family." She stopped, biting at her lips, blinking back tears.

"You are, Aideen. Please call us Riordan and Naomi. We would like that." He paused, his eyes raising to his son, seeing a shadow in his eyes. "Now, I understand breakfast is in order. Naomi?"

"Right here, love, as soon as you've made the tea. Reilly, beside your wife. Redmond and Ryanne are still away and Regan headed into the office. So it's just us four."

Aideen listened to the talk around her before her head began to nod. She didn't hear the soft exclamation from Reilly, just felt him gather her close and walk up the stairs to their bedroom, laying her down and reaching for a quilt to cover her. He sat on the side of the bed, watching for a few minutes, before he quietly shut the door and headed back to the kitchen. He knew his father would want answers and he really wasn't sure what to say.

Riordan looked up as Reilly hesitated in the doorway and his heart ached for his son. This was not how this was to go, was it, Lord? Then he paused. No, maybe it was Your will, Lord. We never know how You will work. We just need to trust and sometimes that is so hard.

Reilly sank back into his chair, reaching for the mug of coffee his mother handed him with a quick thanks before locking up at his father, seeing the compassion there.

"First, Reilly, before we talked, let me pray for you and Aideen. I know you didn't make this move lightly or without prayer."

"No, I didn't, Dad, but I'm not sure Aideen was ready."

His parents shared a look, a look that said Aideen had been ready. but would either one of the younger couple be ready when the ones after her were caught and Reilly went to set her free?

Chapter 10

Reilly looked up at his father finally, not sure how to proceed. Riordan had risen and left the room for a moment, coming back with a stack of files and his laptop.

"Dad? What news do you have?"

"First, Reilly, tell me what your thoughts were yesterday."

Reilly shrugged, his eyes on his mug. "I don't know that I really thought it through, and that's not me. You know that, Dad. I just wanted to keep her safe. She crumbled when she heard about her brother and her parents. Before I go on, I think we need to look into them closer. There's something odd there."

"There is, son. I've done just that. But continue."

Reilly looked at his mother, seeing her watching him closely. "I prayed, Dad, and prayed about this. God didn't say no. Rather I got the feeling from Him that I should. I can't explain that. When I talked to Aideen, she didn't want to at first. She's so afraid we'll be hurt because of her. I have no idea what her home life was like, but it certainly wasn't how we were raised." He paused, taking a sip of coffee. "She did agree but I know she's hesitant about the danger."

Riordan nodded. "How did she take the news about her family?"

"She was shocked, saddened, but somehow I don't think she was too surprised. I can't explain that at all."

"No, I don't think you can. But how are you feeling? Knowing you've taken this step and your bride is still in danger. With Rory and Leah, they weren't married and still faced danger."

"I really don't know, Dad. Right now, I think I'm just so tired. Being on guard all that time like that, it's worn on me, not just physically. I just don't think I can go out any more. I don't have it in me."

"I have a plan I would like to talk to you about, but first about your lady." He reached for the top folder, opened it for a moment, and then passed it over to Reilly. "This is Adam's file. He was not a nice person. I'm glad he didn't get his hands on Aideen."

"Me, too. She told me he killed her animals when she was young, blaming her. He even killed a kitten right in front of her."

"Oh, Reilly! How sad!" His mother spoke for the first time. "We need to help her heal."

"She's hurting, Mom, and doesn't like to show it. I've had to drag things from her." Reilly turned his attention back to his father. "What else, Dad?"

Riordan pointed at the folder. "In there. It lists what all he was involved with. A bit of a nasty person, as my Dad would say. I doubt Aideen realized how deep into crime he was."

"She knew, Dad. Somehow, she knew. She was terrified when I found her."

Naomi began to laugh and the two men stared at her. "Sorry, Reilly. Regan told me how she would switch between your names, depending on what she was saying. She's good for you and you for her."

Reilly grinned "That she did. She used my last name if she was ticked off with me." He shot a look behind him at the door. "How much do we tell her?"

"As much as we feel we need to, at this point." Riordan picked up another folder. "Now, this is where we stand. The men who are now after you are connected to a mob. I'm still digging into that one. Why they are after you, that we're working on as well. We have no idea how much danger you are in from them, but we have to act as if you were."

"Do they think she has something of Adam's? Or that she knows something?"

"That's likely. It wasn't pretty the scene the police walked into when they found Adam. I won't go into details, but it seems he was tortured to some extent. If, as you say, he blamed his sister of the death of his pets, I would suspect he's passed blame onto her."

Reilly had paled, knowing what his father wasn't saying. "She's still in grave danger, isn't she?"

Riordan nodded. "She is and now so are you. I'm trying to find out more information, but it's not readily forthcoming. I have feelers in to some of my contacts to find out what I can. For now, I would suggest you two stay here, not moving outside the fence. I've had Redmond go over the security and enhance it as much as he can."

"Thanks, Dad." Reilly turned as he heard footsteps on the stairs and rose, going to find Aideen.

Naomi looked after him. "What aren't you saying, Riordan?"

"I just don't know, Naomi. I just don't know how well we can protect her. And protect Reilly as well."

Reilly reached for Aideen's hand, drawing her with him to the back deck and to the swing there. Seated, he shifted in his seat, starting the swing, and watching her.

"Did you sleep well?"

She blushed. "I'm sorry, Reilly. I've never done that before. I need to apologize to your parents."

He shook his head, a smile in place. "No, I don't think so. They understand only too well."

She sighed, her head going back as she looked up at the sky. "Why, Reilly? Why is this happening? Where is God in all this?"

He paused, not quite sure what to answer, not wanting to give a pat answer. "To be truthful, Aideen? I'm not sure, but I know He is. I have never doubted that."

"It feels like He has abandoned me. Why?"

"It's like that sometimes. Our lives go through dark patches, patches where we feel all alone."

She nodded. "It doesn't make it any easier." She looked past him at the door. "What has your father come up with?"

"And how did you know that?"

She shrugged. "Knowing you and how you would dig until you unearthed everything you needed, I thought that's what your father would do. So, what did he find out?"

Reilly sighed, knowing he had to talk with her and dreading it. "Dad found out that there was a mob connection to your brother's death."

She snorted, drawing his eyes to her face. "Of course, there is. He ran with the mob. Didn't that come through?"

"I have no idea. I think Dad suspected something like that. But why would you say that?"

"Because I found pictures he dropped one time he broke into my house. And yes, he had a habit of doing that. I had security in place, and he still was in and out before anyone responded. Not one person believed me that it was him. They refused to look at the pictures. They told me it couldn't have been him, it had to be someone who looked like him."

"I see. That's not happening now, Aideen. Dad knows that you're the victim here." He reached for her hand and led her back to the kitchen and to a chair.

Riordan looked up at her and then at Reilly. "Aideen, are you okay?"

She nodded, her hand reaching for Reilly's. "I think so. Reilly mentioned something that you found."

"He did, did he?" Riordan sat back, his eyes assessing her. "I did. Now to explain it. There are some things I can't, part of our investigation that we will have to turn over to the police."

"I'm sorry. An investigation? I thought you just protected people."

"We do that, but there are times we look into events and people. This is one time we're going all out."

"Please, not on my account." Aideen was shaking her head at him.

"Aideen, I will only say this once. Please understand that you are part of our family, however it happened. You always will be. Reilly chose you and that is driving this.   We want this over for both of you." He held up a hand as she went to protest. "No, no words, please.   Just let us work our magic or follow as the Lord leads "

He rose to take a call that he had no choice not to. Reilly watched him walk away and then brought his eyes back to Aideen, seeing the fear and stress in them. He made a sound and then pulled her to her feet, leading her from the kitchen and to the backyard, and then to a swing near the house. He made her sit and then sat himself, setting the swing in motion, an arm around her. He waited, knowing at some point she would speak. She had been too quiet.

Chapter 11

Waiting for Reilly to speak, Aideen thought through what had been going on in her life over the last few months. She was afraid, she thought, more afraid than se had ever been. So why now was this fear so prominent? She shook her head as she felt Reilly's hand on her hair.

"It's tough, I know, my love. Let us help you."

"You've done so much already, Reilly. Too much. How do I let you do more? And the more you search, the more danger you're in."

"You just like using that word, don't you?" He grinned at her frown. "More. You kept repeating it."

She shook her head at him. "You know what I mean, Reilly. How can I take from you?"

"You're not taking. We're giving. It's who we are, my love." He stretched out his legs, his arm still around her. "Let me phrase it this way. If it had been Regan or Ryanne facing what you did, and someone had offered to step in as I did, my family would have been grateful. They may not have liked how it was done, but they would accept it as God leading the way and worked with it."

"Does your family really believe that?"

"We do." Reilly watched her face. "Now, what do we do with you?"

"Put me to work, please. I can't sit around. My mind needs to be occupied." She stared at him. "What? You don't believe that?"

"Oh, I do. I was just trying to think of where we could use your talents." He rose, pulling her to her feet. "Let's go ask Mom. She's a fountain of wisdom and will have an idea."

Reilly stood in the office doorway late that afternoon. He had spent the day with Riordan, sorting through the information flying in to them. He needed a break and had searched the house and grounds for Aideen, finally tracking her down.

Naomi looked up with a smile and beckoned him in. "Your wife has a real talent here, son."

"And that would be?" He perched on the arm of her chair, his hand running down her hair to rest on her shoulder.

She looked up, relaxed for once, a smile on her face. "Your Mom has such a wealth of photographs, Reilly. She wanted someone to sort through them with her, and you have all been so busy, she hasn't asked." She caught a look on his face and sighed. "I know. I shouldn't done this."

"No, Aideen, I'm glad you did." He reached to pick up one of the five siblings. "What age were we in this picture, Mom? Rory about 13?"

She looked over. "That would be about right. Aideen has been such a help. She's been able to get to know our family in a way that words can't tell her. It's more than a day's work, that's for sure." She rose. "It's nearing dinnertime, isn't it? Did your Dad pull anything for us?"

"No, I don't think he did, Mom, but if you have meat and veggies for the grill, I can take care of that."

Naomi reached to drop a kiss on his cheek. "Thank you, son. We could use some of your grill work." She walked away, leaving Aideen staring after her.

"You grill?" At his nod, she sighed. "What other talents are you hiding?"

He grinned at her and then reached to draw her to her feet. "A lot. Come and help me."

She shook her head. "I need to talk to your Dad for a moment. Where would he be?"

Reilly started to laugh, bringing a frown to her face. "I'm sorry, but he always hangs around the grill whenever one of us is grilling. He says it's quality time with us. We think he's afraid we'll burn dinner."

She laughed, then tucked her arm into his elbow. "Then, let's go find him. Who all is here for dinner anyway?"

He shrugged. "Us four, likely Regan. I thought I hear Redmond and Ryanne come in, so likely them as well." He felt her hand tighten on his arm. "Don't worry. They'll love you."

"That's easy for you to say." She stood watching as he pulled meat and veggies from the fridge. "Here. What do you want to do with the veggies?"

He turned, surprise on his face. No one usually offered to help the other cooking. "Cleaned, I think, and then sliced or chopped however you want. There's foil in the drawer beside you."

Reilly stood and watched as Aideen moved around the kitchen, wonder on his face. Lord, is she for real? I know my sisters help and all, but this is different. Thank you for her.

Later that night, Redmond approached Reilly as he stood, a coffee mug in hand, and stopped beside him.

"Reilly, we need to talk at some point."

Reilly shot him a look and nodded. "About what you found?"

Redmond nodded. "About that. I did some digging while we were watching the old farmhouse. I found some interesting material on her brother."

"I can imagine it's interesting. How deep?"

"Deep. I don't think she realizes just all he was involved with."

"She knows. She just hasn't said yet. She's not sure if she can totally trust us." He shot a look at his brother. "She's dropped a few words here and there."

"She does? Then we really do need to talk to her."

"We will, at some point. Just not right now. She's lost her brother, her parents, and even though there were issues there, she is still grieving. To say nothing of running for her life and then marrying."

"Yea, about that. Are you sure?"

Reilly looked up to see Aideen standing in front of him and knew that she had heard Redmond's question. He reached to pull her to him. "Absolutely, Redmond. Absolutely. I have no doubt on God's leading in that."

Redmond studied his brother and then Aideen, before he nodded. "Aideen, I apologize for my question. If I was out of line, please forgive me. You two are well suited for each other." He surprised her with a quick kiss on her cheek before he walked away.

"Reilly?"

"What, my love? Redmond? He's just checking in with me to make sure I was okay. It's what we do."

"I can see that. Listen, is it okay if I retire? It's been a long few days."

"Sure." He set his mug down and then turned her to the house. "Come on. I'll walk you up."

Chapter 12

Reilly stood watching his father, waiting for him to finish his conversation with Rory. Rory had called, asking questions as to what was going on. Riordan's eyes were on Reilly, a frown in place.

"Dad? What did Rory say?" Reilly had barely waited until his father laid his phone down.

"Somehow, they've discovered Leah's place and have been asking questions. He says it's slow right now, so they're closing for a couple of weeks and heading here."

"I don't like that."

"No, none of us do." Riordan paused, his eyes on his phone before he looked back up at Reilly. "No, don't blame yourself or Aideen. She did nothing to bring this on. It's deeper than we thought. Not like with Leah and her tin boxes and maps and hidden rooms and staircases."

"No, it's not. This seems too deep. Dad, I think there's more to it than what we've uncovered. They have to think she has something of his."

"I know. And she denies it. She said she refused to take anything from him or from her parents. I sent a team to her house and they searched, sending her photos to look at. She found nothing out of the ordinary. She doesn't have a lot."

"No, she doesn't. She's been on the move too much, trying to stay hidden from her brother." Riordan sat back in his chair, his finger tapping on a file folder. "Has she said much about her childhood?"

"No, she hasn't. Other than that he killed her pets, blamed her, and terrorized her the whole time. Oh, and that her parents always took Adam's side. Never believed her, she said."

"I can only imagine what her childhood was like." He looked up as he heard footsteps. "Aideen, come on in. We need your help."

Aideen appeared in the doorway before she walked to where Reilly stood, a hand out for her. "You do? What with?"

"Sit." He watched as she sat carefully, not leaning back on the chair. "Relax, Aideen. I just need to talk to you about what we've found."

"What you haven't found, you mean. What do they think I have of Adam's? I refused anything he tried to give me. If I found he had left something, I pitched it into the garbage. So if they want to find it, they can go dig through all the landfill sites in every place I've lived." She stared at Riordan, seeing him shake his head. "Yes, it's that bad. Adam tried to get me to take ornaments, books, pictures for him. I refused. He knew I wanted nothing from him. I would come home and find parcels at my door. I knew it was from him and they just got thrown away, unopened. I didn't want anything from him." She frowned, her brow furrowed as she thought. "My parents tried the same thing, but I refused anything from them. What your team found in my apartment is what I have gathered myself. I didn't have a lot. I was always on the move, staying just a step or two ahead of him."

Reilly studied her. "Then how did he know you found material on him?"

She shook her head. "He shouldn't have but I imagine they had to turn it over to his lawyers. I just happened on it one day. He had been around, trying to get in. I found a file he dropped when he left. I was going to throw it out but took a peek at it. That's when I went to the police. They tried to shove me off, but I persisted and when a detective finally looked at it, they were all set to take Adam to trial. I didn't understand what was written. I'm not into financial stuff and that's what it was."

"That's what we've heard they are looking for. We've put word out that you have nothing, that you didn't read the material, and just turned it over to the police. I have no idea what lies ahead for you, testifying now. Adam's case is closed, but I'm told they're working on finding who he worked for. This is when it becomes dangerous for you, my dear. That's why we need to keep you close to one of us and here at the house as much as possible." He held up a hand at her protest. "I know. It's restricting your movements, yours and Reilly. Reilly stays with you as he has been."

"But he needs to work. You need him at the office." Aideen turned to Reilly, a desperate look on her face.

"No, I'm working from home. What I do now I can do from anywhere. Dad has it set up here that I can. I look after our contracts, so that's not a problem. There is no way I'm leaving you on your own."

Riordan ducked his head to hide a smile at the battle of wills between the younger couple, not sure who would win. He prayed that Reilly would. Aideen was good for him, he thought. She challenges him but doesn't belittle him. She listens to what he has to say but responds in her own unique way. He laughed to himself at the number of times he had heard her calling him by his last name, then switching in the next sentence to his first name. Regan had laughed when she told them about that.

Naomi had doubted that had happened until she heard it for herself.

Aideen finally sighed. "Okay, I guess I'm stuck here for now. Just solve this and solve it quickly, please? Reilly needs to get on with his life."

Reilly opened his mouth to speak, then snapped it closed. *Lord, she's not ready yet, is she? Not ready to hear I don't want to walk away from her, to give her the freedom she deserves and has never had. Lord, bring healing to my lady and peace that only You can bring.*

Aideen turned to Riordan, eyes narrowed as she watched his face. "What do we do now?"

"For now, Naomi really does want your help with that project of hers. And before you tell me you're taking her away from work, she has wanted to cut back her hours and has for a while. Now that the five are home to stay, she can. She was delighted with her time spent with you yesterday." He looked behind Aideen. "In fact, here she is, looking for you, I suspect."

Aideen stared at him for a moment before she arose, excusing herself. Reilly had to cover a quick grin at her muttered words of leaving them to work out her problem without her and why would they need her for that any way.

Riordan had caught her words as well and shook his head, before looking at Reilly, seeing the mirth in his son's eyes, something he hadn't seen in months, he realized. His heart broke, knowing his children were hurting and that for once he could not make it all better for them, not like when they were young.

"Reilly, now what do we do with you?"

"I'll work from here, Dad, but I do want to do some research into her brother. Something is still not ringing true with what we know."

"I know, and that disturbs me. There's something about the whole thing I need to look into. I have Aideen's identification and want to look into that. It just seems strange how they treated her all her life."

Riordan studied his son for a moment before he spoke, putting into words what they both dreaded. "You're thinking adoption?"

Reilly nodded. "At the very least. Abduction is something else I want to check out. When I looked at her birth certificate, there was something odd about it." He sighed. "I just hope it was legitimate. I don't think I'll get her to go through another ceremony."

"But you may have to. We'll work it out." Riordan rose, leaving his son in the office, deep in thought before he too rose and headed for a work station, signing in and starting his search

Chapter 13

Naomi stood for a moment, watching Reilly at work, before she approached him, his head rising as she did.

"Mom? Is something wrong? Is it Aideen?" He shoved his chair back, ready to stand until his mother's hand on his shoulder stopped him.

"No, it's not that. She's fine. She's wonderful, in fact. She's bringing out your fun side again. Neither your father or I realized how deep you had shoved it." She sat, her eyes assessing him. "No, it's just something she said and I think you need to know about it."

Reilly shot a look at the door and then back at his mother. "Where is she?"

"In the living room. She found that old diary of your Gran's and is totally engrossed in it." She paused, not quite sure how to continue. "Did you know she just finished high school and then ran? She has never been to college, never had a chance for anything like normalcy for someone her age?"

"I suspected that. She never came out and said it. Now what, Mom? What do we do to help her?" Reilly sighed, sorrow flickering across his face. "And I rushed her into a marriage when she wasn't ready either."

"Don't beat yourself up over that. If God had not meant you to do that, He would have put roadblocks in your way." She looked behind her at the door. "No, it's not that, son. It's something she said about one of Adam's friends. That's what concerns me." She looked down at the paper she held and then laid it on the desk. "This is the name she gave. She mentioned other names as well. I could hear the fear in her voice when she spoke of them. I think she was on the run from more than her brother."

"I know she was, just from what little she's said. Thanks, Mom." He looked at his mother before he looked down at the paper, not reading the words. "I think we need to pack up her place and that means taking her on a trip across the province. Can we arrange that somehow?"

His mother shook her head. "Your Dad and I talked about that. He's going to send a team, Redmond with them, with authorization from Aideen to close her apartment and anything else she needs closed down. That way, she's not at risk."

Reilly sighed and then blew out a breath. "I was worried about that very thing, Mom. Thank you." He watched as she rose and walked away before he looked down at the paper. His hand froze in its movements of rubbing at it and he stared once more at the door.

Aideen, my love, what have you become involved in? I feel like we're on the edge of a hurricane and getting sucked into it whether we want to or not. He turned to his computer, his fingers flying as he typed in names.

Three hours later he rose and stretched, his eyes going to the clock. It was past lunch time realized, no one having disturbed him. He headed for the kitchen, papers in hand, and stopped. Aideen sat at the table, her hands wrapped around a mug, a look of lostness and loneliness on her face. He slid down beside her, arm around drawing her to him.

She turned, startled, to study him. "Reilly? Where have you been?"

"In the office. Mom gave me some names."

She sighed. "I thought she would. Your Mom is good at getting people to talk, you know." She sounded disgruntled at that.

Reilly grinned for a moment before he gave into impulse and dropped a kiss on her temple, bringing her eyes back to him, a question in them. "She is. We could never hide anything from her, and believe me, we tried hard when we were kids."

She smiled, the smile not quite reaching her eyes. "Where do we go from here, Reilly? I mean, I can't stay here forever. It's not fair to your parents or your siblings. Or you." She refused to look at him.

"For now, we stay put. Don't think of running from me, Aideen. I would only come after you."

"You wouldn't!" She studied his face once more, and then spoke softly. "You would. Reilly, what am I to do with you?"

"Stay with me. Let me help you. Let my family help you." He turned his heads as he heard voices and then reached for her hand and drew her to her feet and out to the back deck where he settled them into the wicker loveseat. "We really want to help you, to solve this, to give you a life that you've never had."

She nodded, her eyes on the horizon, watching the birds, the insects, the bees, looking anywhere but at him. She knew what he was saying, his words having a deeper meaning that what they seemed.

"Where is God in this, Reilly? Please remind me."

His arm tightened around her. "He's here, my love. He is right here with us. He has promised to never leave us or forsake us. He is the strong tower we can run to. He covers you with His wings and provides a place of rest, of comfort, of protection. And no, I'm not just saying words. I have felt Him in so many ways over the years. I know I told you we would go into countries, find people and bring them out. That is so dangerous, especially in some countries. There have been times we have had to go into deep hiding before we could make a break out. God has been there, protecting us, shutting eyes and mouths and ears. Our teams have experienced God in a way not many do."

She searched his face. "You mean that, don't you? How do I find that?"

"You already have. Sometimes He provides people, like us, for that. I'm not saying you're out of danger, not by a long shot. But with our resources, we're working hard to find who it is." He looked down and then back to the kitchen. "I do need to talk to you about some of the names."

He felt the shudders running through her and prayed for his lady. He knew he loved her deeply and that was not something he had expected to feel. He dreaded the day she would walk away from him.

"Which one? Tom Ames?"

Reilly sighed. "That's the one. How close was he to your brother?"

She turned to watch the horizon again, a frown on her face as she thought it through. "I'm not really sure, Reilly. I avoided him as much as I could. I didn't feel comfortable around him, not when I heard how he treated other girls. He destroyed lives." She stopped, unable to continue. "I always thought he was into human trafficking. Girls would be there, and then just disappear. I would never hear of them again. I know he did drugs. I saw him and ran as fast as I could after that. I think he was helping Adam try and find me."

"He's into that and much more. The police are looking for him and have tracked him to the last town Adam was in. That's how close he was to you." He paused, knowing he had to continue and not wanting to. "I had someone contact me, an informant we use at times. He let me know that if I came across you, I was to put you somewhere you couldn't be found. Apparently, this Ames is after you for revenge. He didn't take it kindly when you ran. He's been trying to get to you and has been thwarted on many occasions."

"It was him?" Her face crumpled as fear took over.

Reilly gave a sound of anger and swept her into his arms, holding tight as she wept. "It was him. What did he do?"

She shook her head. "I thought it was Adam. Someone broke into one of my apartments and left flowers and chocolate and a dress. That dress was horrible, Reilly. I can't even begin to describe how it disgusted me. It was something like someone on the streets would wear. I couldn't see Adam doing that, but I didn't know."

Reilly's face tightened at the thought of what she had been through, his gaze meeting his father's and then Rory's, seeing their eyes narrow and a stern, hard look come across his face. Rory nodded and spun on his heel, heading for the office. He would look until he found everything he could on the man threatening his brother's wife.

Riordan sat quietly down in a chair near the young couple, a look of compassion on his face, his heart raised in prayer, his mind racing as to what the next steps were. He watched Reilly's face and then nodded. Reilly was deeply in love, he thought, whether Aideen felt the same way or not. He would do everything he could to protect her, and Riordan

knew his son well enough to know he would put his
life on the line for her.

89

Chapter 14

Rory went looking for Reilly later that day, finding him pacing the yard. He stopped for a moment, remembering how Reilly and Leah had disappeared on them and they had to hunt for them. Lord, please, don't let this happen to him again. Don't let him go through what I went through.

Reilly looked up as Rory approached him, a grin lighting up his face. "I didn't know you had come yet." He looked around him. "Where's Leah and your little one?"

"In the house. Mom won't let Leah near our daughter. She's in her glory." Rory grinned as the picture of his mother and her granddaughter filled his vision for a moment.

"She is that." Reilly paused and then spoke. "What did you find, Rory? I can tell you did."

"It's not good, Reilly. She was right about him. They're looking for him, in fact they have the house where he is surrounded at the moment. He's what she couldn't say and much more. I'm glad you kept her safe."

Reilly's eyes slid shut. "I knew it. I just had a feeling when she was talking." His eyes opened. "Is she safe then?"

Rory shook his head. "No, not by a long shot. Whoever Adam angered, they want her for revenge. They don't care if he's dead." He paused, not sure how to continue. "Her parents were part of it, Reilly. They were part of what he was involved with. I have spoken with the police investigator and received a partial report, all he would give me. They were executed."

Reilly's breath caught in his throat. "That's about what I figured. Now I have to tell her."

Rory's hand on his arm stopped him. "Dad's talking to her. He felt he should, rather than you. His words to me were that we would be the bearers of bad news, you would be her comforter."

Reilly stared at his brother. "There is no way Dad said that." When Rory just shook his head, Reilly's hand rubbed at the back of his neck. "He didn't, did he?"

Rory grinned. "He did. He and Mom have come to care deeply for your wife." He shook his head. "I can't get used to that, you married."

"Don't get too used to that. I promised her I would set her free when this was all over." Reilly walked away at that, leaving Rory staring after him.

"I don't think so, brother. Not from what I've seen. You love her. And I know she loves you. I can see it in how she talks about you."

Aideen looked up as Reilly sat beside her, tears on her face. She reached for him and he hugged her tight, his eyes on her head before he looked up at his father.

"Dad?" He frowned when his father just shook his head. "What happened?"

"Her family, that's what." Riordan was angry at her family and knew he had to deal with that. "To treat her like that." He reached for a folder, handing it to Reilly. "Here. Read through this and then talk to your wife. Come find me when you're done."

Reilly nodded, his attention not on the folder as he set it aside, but on Aideen.

"Aideen? Oh, my love, please talk to me."

She looked at him, wonder in her heart at what he called her. Was she really, she thought? Am I really his love? Oh, Lord, I wish it was so true. He's a courageous, strong, Godly man, someone I need in my life. But I know he's going to let me walk away when this is over. And as much as I wish it was over, I don't want him to leave him. Not ever.

"What do you want me to say?" She pointed to the folder. "What have you gone and dug up now?"

He laughed at her and then sobered, catching a light in her eyes he hadn't seen before. Lord, I don't want to let her go, but she needs her freedom. Please guide my steps and my words.

"Dad did. He handed me this, didn't tell me what was in it, and told me to talk to you. He said something about your family."

She gave an unladylike snort at that. "What family? After seeing yours, I realize I wasn't a member of a family. I was just someone who lived in that house. They weren't a family. Never were. But what has he dug up? And do I want to know?"

"He seemed to think you needed to." He paused, a prayer rising to his lips, before he opened the folder.

Aideen leaned against him as he opened the folder, her eyes on the photo, a shadow in them. "Those are my parents. But I don't look much like them, do I?" She turned her eyes to Reilly. "Did I even belong to them?"

"I'm sure Dad has looked into that very possibility. Here, let's lay these on the table as we go through them." He pulled the coffee table closer, and turned as she gave a sound of dismay. "It's okay,

Aideen. Really it is. It gets moved all the time." He waited, a frown on his face. "Were you never allowed to move anything?"

She shook her head. "Never. Everything had to stay in the place it was put in. Furniture, ornaments, books. I was never allowed to touch anything other than what I really had to. What kind of life is that?" She looked away from him, biting at her lip, tears near the surface. "I missed out on so much."

"You did. Let us help you, please." He reached for her hand, squeezing it before he reached for the next paper in the folder. "Now, this is interesting."

"What is it?"

"Your parents' marriage certificate. There's a difference in the names, though." He hunted for a pen and paper and then was up, running to the office for them and back to his seat beside her, handing them to her. "Here. You make notes on what we find."

"And why would I do that, Stuart?"

He grinned at her. "Back to that, are we? Because if we make notes on any discrepancies we find, we may just come across the big picture and figure out what's going on."

She nodded. "Okay, so to start with, the names. That's strange, you know." Her eyes stayed on the certificate as he watched her. "I can remember they using these names, when I was small. Just for a while and then I was told I had to use another name. Why?"

"Put that down. A memory we can search through as we go along." He handed her the next sheet.

She frowned and turned to him. "Where is your Dad finding this stuff? This is a picture of Adam as a child. I can remember seeing it and then it disappeared. I have no idea where. Is he not their son?"

"We think he is, but we are working to confirm that."

"This next one, what is that?" She pointed at it. "It looks like a deformed home. What is it?"

Reilly studied it and then looked at his father's note. "It says it was your father's home as a child. By the looks of it, it has really fallen into disrepair. Did you ever see it?"

She shook her head. "Never. I never heard anything about their childhood. They never spoke of it. In fact, they hardly talked to me at all. I was raised by a nanny, I think. But then, she could have been anyone. She disappeared with I was fourteen or fifteen. When I asked about her, they told me she had moved on and wouldn't be back." She paused, sadness on her face before a look of horror crossed it. "Did they kill her?"

"We can look into that. Put her name down, will you? How much time did you spend with her?"

Aideen sat back, her eyes staring into the distance. "Not a lot, you know. Not what you would expect. She got me up in the morning, got me dressed, fed me breakfast and then I didn't see her again until the afternoon. She was there while I had my dinner, had me get ready for bed early, and then left. I would say about four hours in a day." She turned to him. "That's not long for someone who's supposed to be taking care of you."

"No, it's not. Did she ever say anything?"

Aideen went to shake her head, then paused. "One time, not long before she left, she asked me something. Now what was it? I think Mother overheard and it wasn't long afterwards that she left." She turned horrified eyes on him. "She asked me if I had ever thought about being a lost child. Why would she say that?"

"We'll figure it out. Now, this next photo."

She touched it, a longing on her face. "This was the woman I called Grandmother. Now, I'm not even sure if she was. She loved me, she told me that. She helped me in so many ways, but the most important way was her faith. She led me to where I am today. I can still hear her prayers and her repeating verses. She died when I was nine or ten. I miss her."

"Put down her name as well." Reilly studied his bride, sensing she was wearing down but knowing better than to ask her to quit. She would only refuse, he knew.

He paused at the next paper, wondering what his father had been thinking. He handed her the map of the area, their house marked, and then a house down the road marked as well. He watched as she studied it and then her eyes slid closed.

"We lived there, Reilly. We lived in that house. For about a year, I think. It was when I was ten or so." She suddenly turned to him. "You're the one!"

"I'm the one what?"

"I can remember getting lost in a store one day, not able to find my parents. I had started to panic, not able to see them, and I couldn't find the doors to the store. I was so afraid. Not afraid of being lost but of what would happen. You. You're the one who approached me and led me to the front door. You waited with me until I saw my mother heading towards me and I made you leave. She was angry, I could tell, and I didn't want you hurt."

"I remember. I didn't know that was you. I always wondered what happened to you." He reached to brush a hand down her cheek and then set the papers aside, reaching for her hand and drawing her to her feet. "Let's walk in the yard for a while, Aideen. We both need a break from this."

"We do." Her hand nestled into his and she felt his strength in his grip.

They walked the yard, hand in hand, not speaking, content just to be with one another. They didn't see Rory and Leah standing on the deck watching them.

"What's her story, Rory?" Leah was concerned about Reilly.

"It's not pretty, Leah. We're still trying to figure out what's going on. Dad said her brother was after her for turning him into the police. Then they find him dead and their parents dead. Word is out on the streets that the mob is after her. We're trying to find out why and protect her at the same time." Rory's arms tightened around his wife. "We have no idea where this will lead."

"Just like with me. I thought I was in danger, but this is far more than we ever faced." She looked up at him. "But what if the mob isn't after her at all? Did you think through that possibility?"

Rory stared down at his wife, stunned at how quickly she had gone to the centre of their dilemma. "I hadn't but I'm sure Dad has." He nodded towards his brother. "I don't want to see either one of them hurt and I'm just afraid that's what will happen."

"I am too, Rory." She turned as she heard their daughter. "I need to see to Esther. Watch them for me, Rory? Make sure nothing happens to them."

Rory watched her walk away, a frown in place. Now, what did she mean by that?

A sudden noise in the air had him looking up, then shouting for Reilly and Aideen, his feet hitting the lawn as he ran towards them.

Reilly looked up as he heard his brother's voice and then heard the sound of an incoming model plane. He grabbed for Aideen's hand and pulled her with him as he raced for the house. Unable to make it in time, he hit the ground, his body covering hers as gunfire erupted from the plane. Afterwards, neither man could say what had actually happened. All they knew is that when the plane disappeared, Reilly lay, bloodied, his bride still beneath him.

Chapter 15

Riordan hit the back deck on the run, stopping for a moment to yell for Naomi to call for help, and then hit the yard, racing for his son. Rory was already on his knees, his hands trying to find a pulse on his brother and then on Aideen.

"Rory?" He could hear the fear in his father's voice.

"They're alive, Dad. I don't know how. Reilly's been hit but I don't know about Aideen." He looked around as Redmond appeared at his side. "Redmond, if Dad and I can lift Reilly up enough, can you and Regan move Aideen away from him? I don't know if she's been hit and we need to find out. Ryanne, you're on the gate."

Ryanne ran for the gate, hearing the sirens approaching. She quickly hit the access code and watched as the gate swung open, letting the emergency personnel in. She looked around and then closed the gate, knowing she had to stay where she was, yet desperate to hear Reilly's condition.

The paramedics dropped their kits and reached for gloves, turning to the young couple, listening as Rory explained to the responding officers what had happened.

"A model plane? Gunfire?" The officer didn't believe him at first until Rory turned on him, a fine anger in his voice

"Yes. A model plane. Gunfire. I know what I saw and heard. Now, find the ones responsible. And just pray it's not a murder investigation." He stood, his father's arm around him, his hands covered with his brother's blood, knowing that Leah and Naomi would be watching from the deck.

He didn't hear his father speak to Redmond or see him run for first the house and then for Ryanne. Regan crowded close to her father and his arm encircled her as well. They watched in silence at the desperate pace the emergency personnel were working at, finally loading the two stretchers into the ambulance and heading for the nearest hospital, the family running for their vehicles to follow, locking the gate behind them, leaving the police to search. They knew one of their employee would be there, to watch and assist.

Rory paced the waiting room, Redmond keeping pace with him on one side, his sisters on the other. Leah and his parents were huddled in a corner. He could see the anger in his father, knew he had been on the phone with his office. It was taking too long, he thought.

The physician who emerged from the rooms hesitated for a moment, then approached Riordan. Riordan knew him from church and rose to shake his head.

"Peter? What news?"

"I'm the one treating your daughter-in-law, I guess she is. She's fortunate. It looks as if Reilly protected her well. When he took her down, she hit hard and knocked herself out. She's coming around but we want to keep her in overnight."

"We're posting guards and don't tell me we can't." Riordan's anger was in his voice as he sought to control it.

"I wouldn't expect anything else. James is treating Reilly. He said he'd be out shortly." He shook his head. "I'm sorry. I don't know his status.

Just know that we're praying for you. Emily, our charge nurse, was able to get word to the pastor and he said he'd start the prayer chain working."

"Thank you, Peter." Riordan sank back down, his arm around Naomi, as the rest of his family crowded close.

"No word yet, Dad?"

Riordan shook his head. "Peter's not treating Reilly. Aideen is okay, thank God, for that."

They agreed and then turned in unison as they heard footsteps heading their way. James Archer, a fellow church member, stood there, a grim look on his face.

Riordan was on his feet. "James? Please. Tell me he's still alive."

James' face cleared. "He is. Sorry, I didn't mean to frighten you, although with all that blood I'm sure you were. He's been hit twice. Once in the shoulder, once in the abdomen. Both have bled heavily but we're not seeing any real damage. It looks as if the bullets went through. We'll be taking him to surgery to stitch him up. Probably about two hours or so. We'll take you up to the surgical waiting room." He looked at Naomi as she rose.

"James? I want to go back to Aideen. Please. She has no family."

"Aideen?" He was puzzled.

"That's right. No one outside of the family knows. She's Reilly's wife. Peter must have known from her name." She turned puzzled eyes on Peter as he stood just outside their circle.

"I wondered, Naomi. It was a guess on my part when I treated her. I hope I didn't step over any boundaries."

"No, you haven't. This is just so new for us all. Reilly hasn't said yet how much he wants word to get out."

Peter nodded as he watched Riordan's face. "We'll keep it quiet, at least as quiet as we can. Word will leak out at some point." He looked behind him. "I see some of your people are here as well as the police. It's going to be a long day for you. Come find me if you need anything." Peter and James walked away, back to their duties, but with questions on their mind.

Riordan walked away with Naomi, heading for Aideen. They stopped at her bedside, watching closely as she moved slightly.

"How do we keep her safe now, Riordan? They found them at our place."

"I know, and I would like to know just how they did that. But if they knew who Reilly was, it wouldn't be much of a stretch to find him." Riordan hugged his wife. "I need to go speak with Paul and then I'll be back."

Naomi approached the stretcher Aideen was laying on, her hand reaching to stroke Aideen's face. Now, what, Lord? We've tried to keep them hidden but that didn't work. Protect us while we're here.

She turned as she heard footsteps and Rory and Leah appeared at her side.

"She's really okay, Mom?" Rory's voice was quiet.

"We have no reason not to think so. Now, your brother."

"Redmond's going in with him as is Regan. Ryanne is hovering, not quite sure which room to come to."

Naomi nodded, then turned. "Send her in. You two go check on Riordan, please?"

Hours later, Aideen roused, laying with her eyes closed as she tried to determine just where she was. She felt a hand on her arm and peeked. Naomi? What was going on?

"Aideen? Are you with us?" She heard Naomi's soft voice.

"I am. Where am I? And my head hurts."

Naomi gave a soft laugh. "You knocked yourself out. They're keeping you for the night." She paused. "Do you remember anything?"

Aideen narrowed her eyes and stared at Naomi. "I do. I remember Reilly shoving me to the ground and then nothing more. Where is he?"

"I'm sorry, dear. He was shot protecting you." Naomi was unable to keep Aideen in her bed.

Aideen was up, searching for her clothes and then fleeing to the bathroom. She returned fully clothed, determination of her pale face.

"Take me to him."

"Aideen, you need to rest."

"I won't rest until I see him. How bad?"

"How bad?" Naomi followed her as Aideen headed for the door.

"How bad was he hurt? And just where is he?"

"He's on the surgical floor. They won't let you in. Not at this time of night."

Aideen spun, catching her balance with a hand on the wall. "No, they will let me in. I can be very vocal if I need to be."

She stopped a nurse and then headed for the stairs.

Riordan had approached. "Where is she heading?"

"For her husband. We need to catch up with her."

Riordan nodded. "Redmond's there."

Chapter 16

His eyes flickered open and shut as Reilly tried to rouse, his hand finding his shoulder and then his abdomen at the pain he felt. He finally cracked open his eyes, finding Aideen at his bedside, a hand on his.

"Aideen? You're okay?"

"I am, Reilly. But you're not."

"I can tell that. What happened?"

"What happened? Someone used a model plane to shoot at us. You shoved me down and took the bullets." She paused, her eyes on him. "But which one of us were they meant for?"

"I would hazard a guess that it would be you but they could be after me too. If they get rid of me, they can get to you."

He reached to elevate the head of his bed, grimacing as he did so. "What time is it?"

"About three in the morning. You had surgery yesterday to stitch you up, I'm told." She touched his face. "Reilly, you could have been killed."

"I know. It's who I am, Aideen, and what I do. Do you think I would do any less for my wife than I do for a stranger?" He sighed, his head going back, pain coursing through him for a moment. "How long do I have to stay?"

"They want you to stay in for a couple of days." She watched, a half-smile on her face. "But you won't."

He shook his head. "Who's out there?"

"Outside your door?" At his nod, she studied him. "Redmond and Regan. There's an officer as well."

"Find Redmond. Have him get rid of the officer somehow. No, get Regan to do that. I need Redmond's help."

She hesitated and then headed for the door. "You shouldn't, Reilly. You need to stay."

"No, I need out of here to find out who it was. We've touched a nerve somewhere, I think."

"I know we did, but we need you to have medical care."

He swung his legs off the side of the bed. "We have a doctor on staff. We'll use him." He watched as she still hesitated, her eyes on his face. "Please, Aideen? Just go find Redmond for me. Trust me. I've done this before."

She spun, her eyes huge. "You've been shot before?"

He shook his head, his own eyes narrowing at her concern. "No, just a beating at one time. Shoo, go do what I asked."

She glared at him. "Stuart, you're lucky you're so good looking. I wouldn't do it for anyone else." She was gone before he could reply.

Redmond entered, shooting a glance before him before staring at his brother. "What did she say that has you so shell-shocked?"

Reilly shook his head. "It's between us. Help me, please Redmond. We need to get out of here and now. They'll be coming for her and won't care that it's a public building and others are around."

"Dad figured you'd do this. He's waiting down by the Emergency entrance." He helped his brother to dress and then arm under his, helped him to walk to the door. "We need a wheelchair for you, Reilly."

"No, they'll be looking for that. Where's the service elevator?"

"Right here." Aideen was at his side, her arm around him to support him. "Let's get you home, Reilly."

She stood an hour later, watching as Reilly slept before she took sank down for her sleep, her body worn and battered feeling. She had left the door open for Naomi to bring in the physician and didn't stir as he examined Reilly.

Patrick, the physician, stood in the hallway where he could watch Reilly. "He shouldn't have come home. Not yet. I'll need to get some supplies."

"Aideen couldn't convince him to stay, she said, and she tried. What do we do now, Patrick?"

"We try and keep him still. I can sedate him for a bit, but I don't want to if I can avoid that. I will run an IV and then some pain meds through it. He's going to be really hurting in a day or so."

"He will. What about Aideen?"

"She'll be hurting some. I won't try and give her anything too strong, though." He looked back through the door. "She's not going to leave his side, is she? What's the story there?"

Naomi and Riordan shared a look. "He was on the hunt for her as you know. To keep her safe, he asked her to marry him, with the plan to let her go when this is all over."

Patrick began to shake his head. "That's not happening, not from what I'm seeing."

"We don't think so either, but first we have to find out what is really going on. And that is a real struggle."

"Why?"

"We're not sure if Aideen was ever the biological daughter of the ones she called parents. They and her brother were murdered. Her brother had been after her. Now we're getting all sorts of rumours and scuttlebutt about who's after her now."

"And you have to sort through it all, don't you? My advice? Look for the most innocent one in this." With that, Patrick walked away.

"What did he mean, Riordan?"

Riordan shrugged. "I don't know exactly, but he must have had a reason." Riordan paused. "That folder I gave Reilly. Do you know where it is?"

"I think they left it in the living room yesterday morning when they took a break." Naomi watched as Riordan headed for the stairs in a hurry and disappeared down them before she turned back to her son and his wife.

Reilly pushed himself up in bed two days later, not finding it so hurtful. He watched as Aideen paced the room, muttering to herself, before he held out a hand to her.

"Aideen, come. Sit for a moment."

She stared at him and then his hand before she gave a huge sigh and sat, his hand reaching to touch her hair.

"What is going on, my love?   I know something is."

She nodded, not looking at him. "There is. All this talk about family and who is or isn't related is getting to me. How do I know for sure? Can we even find out?" She finally turned to watch him, a shadow in her eyes.

"I think we can. Dad said he had news for us that he'd share when he was back from the office. He should be here soon." He reached and pulled her close to him, wrapping his arms around her.

Chapter 17

Late that afternoon, Riordan stood and watched as Reilly and Aideen walked towards him through the house. He sighed. Today, he had to shatter a memory or two of Aideen's and he wasn't sure if that was even the right step.

Reilly's steps slowed as he saw his father waiting for them and reached for Aideen's hand, causing her to look up at him. He nodded towards Riordan.

"Dad's home. I don't like the look on his face, though."

Aideen turned to study Riordan and sighed. "What has he discovered now?" She pulled her hand loose and walked towards the older man. "What did you find?"

"Direct and to the point, I see?" He grinned at her, suddenly looking very much like Reilly.

She paused, a frown in place and then turned to look up at Reilly. "Reilly? What's going on? I just had a flash of something?" She stood, shivering, until he wrapped her in his arms.

"Come on, my love. Let's get you sitting down and then see what Dad has to say." He drew her into the office and down on the couch in there. "Dad?"

Riordan pulled over a chair and set the folder he had been carrying down, his eyes on Aideen. "Aideen? What did you just remember?"

She shrugged. "Just something quick, a face that I haven't thought of for years. He looked like my father did, but it wasn't him. Who was it?"

Riordan sighed and reached into the folder, pulling out a photo. He studied it for some time before he handed it to her. "Is this him?"

Aideen kept her eyes on him as she reached for the photo. She gasped when she looked down. "I think it is. Who is it?"

"It's a relative, Aideen, but we're not sure how he's related to you. He's not your father, that much we know. I have Redmond working on that right now. He's hoping to know something in the next few hours." He shared a look with Reilly. "Whatever this is, Aideen, it goes much deeper than just your brother. When you turned him in, something triggered. We're not sure now if they are after you at all. Word on the street is divided on that."

"It is? So, now what?"

"So now what? We look through this material, and try to keep you safe." He held up a hand as she protested. "I know. You don't like the restrictions we've put you under. But if you're out and about, it's not just your life that is at stake. Any innocent person around you is threatened. Do you understand that?" His stern voice brought her startled eyes back to him and she nodded.

"I think I do. What you're saying is that if I go out anywhere, I could be responsible for someone's death."

"To put it succinctly, yes." He looked at Reilly, finding his son studying Aideen, his heart on his face before it shuttered. "Reilly has already been hurt. I would like to prevent that from happening to anyone else."

Aideen stared at him, fear on her face, before she turned to Reilly. "Reilly?"

"Aideen, Dad's right. We need to keep you where you're safe. For now, it's here. Even though they have tracked you down, it will be difficult to get to you." He stared at her until he sensed movement from his father and looked at him. "Dad?"

Riordan looked up from his phone. "That was Redmond. He's on his way in. He has news."

Aideen reached for the folder Riordan held, surprising him. She began to leave through the pages, stopping at a picture of a house. "I know this house. It's the one we lived in when I was about two or three, I think. I remember seeing pictures of it." She raised her eyes, a thoughtful look on her face. "There's something odd about it though. I don't remember the small building to the left. It wasn't there then."

Riordan reached for the photo. "This photo is more modern than what you remember. I'll pull some records and see what I can find." He shared a look with Reilly. "Anything else?"

She searched through the papers, stopping every few moments before shaking her head and moving on. She finally handed him the folder and looked at him. "What was I to be looking for?"

"Anything that would trigger a memory. That one photo did." He watched her face for a moment, his eyes narrowing. "What else did you just remember?"

She glared at him for a moment before she sighed. "Nothing that I can put a finger on. Just impressions of being there when I was young, of other people being there, of moving during the night." She looked up at him, horror on her face.

"Riordan, I think they killed someone that night. Is that why the building is there?"

Riordan nodded slowly, his eyes on Aideen before they moved to Reilly. "That's what we think. Once we can amass enough data, we can ask the police to move in. The thing of it is, Aideen, is that they will think it's you."

She shuddered. "I know they will. I don't like living like this. Do you know what it's like? To have no home? To be on the move all the time? To go from place of employment to another? Do you?"

Reilly tightened his arms around her. "We don't, Aideen, not personally. But we do know from those we've rescued. And you do have a home. Right here." He watched as she turned to stare at him, her eyes narrowed, before she struggled to escape his arms and was up and running from them.

Reilly watched her and then rose, stopping as his father's hand came out.

"Let her go, just for the moment, Reilly. She's grieving so many things and right now, you're mixed up in that grief. She doesn't know what to think or where to turn. That scares her."

Reilly sank back on the couch, his eyes on his father. "You're right, Dad." He ran his hands through his hair. "How do I help her?"

"Just do what you have been doing. Give her space when she needs it."

Redmond approached Aideen later that afternoon and she turned, her face expressionless.

Great, Redmond thought. Dad sends me out to talk with her and she's not ready for that.

"Aideen?"

"What? What now, Redmond? What more bad news?"

He shook his head. "No, I'm not sure if it is or not. I just wanted to talk with you." He pointed towards the side of the yard. "Let's sit, okay? I've literally been on the run all day and my feet hurt."

She looked down at his feet. "I'm sure they do, but barefoot?"

He grinned. "Barefoot. It's how we were allowed to go. I still do. I catch both Mom and Dad doing that."

She sighed as she sat. "I could never do that." She stared at the sneakers on her feet. "I remember trying it once and being severely disciplined for that. That wasn't right, Redmond."

"No, it wasn't." He reached for her feet, pulling off her socks and shoes, despite her protest, and tucking them behind his back.

"Redmond! I can't do this!" She tried to reach behind him and he caught her wrists in a gentle manner.

"I know you feel you can't, but you can. You can leave that garbage in the past and start fresh." He looked up to see Reilly watching from the back patio area. "Reilly was our quiet one but he could think up a lot of games and fun. He still can. What he went through recently changed him."

Aideen studied Redmond's face, seeing something there. "What didn't he tell me?"

"I have no idea. I know he was chewed up and spit out on his last extraction. Then, he and Leah were kidnapped. Now, he's been on the run looking for you for weeks now. He's tired, but he will never stop. Not until you're free of everything."

"But what if I'm never free? What if you never catch the people? I can't live caged like this. And I can't ask Reilly to." Her voice was so quiet Redmond could barely hear her words.

"He made his choice, Aideen, and his choice is you. He doesn't say a lot but he thinks deep."

She snorted at that, causing Redmond to grin. "Doesn't say a lot? I can't get him to stop and let me say anything." She tilted her head to study the younger man. "But there is something you need to tell me."

He nodded. "There is. Dad said you recognized one of the photos but indicated there was only the house, not the little building. We've talked to the police and they've been able to obtain a warrant to go in and search. Apparently, someone else has said the same thing you did."

"Someone else?" Her brow furrowed as she thought it through. "But who?"

"That they haven't said. They're searching even now as we speak." He rose, sensing Reilly walking towards them. "I'm sorry, Aideen. I wish I had better news. But we still need to talk and go back through that paperwork and photos that Dad brought."

"Not tonight, Redmond. Aideen has had enough." Reilly sat beside his wife, reaching for her shoes behind him. "Unless she feels she can."

Aideen stared between the two men and nodded. "I can, but later please?"

"Later." Redmond walked away, leaving the young couple facing each other.

"Did he really take off your shoes?" Reilly tried to smother the grin at her disgruntled look.

"He did. He didn't warn me that was what he was going to do." She reached for her shoes, her hand stopping at the look on his face. "Reilly?"

"He's right. You don't have to wear shoes." He pointed at his own feet. "I'm not."

"You're not?" Her voice rose to a squeak. "I thought he was just talking."

"Redmond teases a lot, but this time, he was right. Come summer, we seldom wear shoes, any of us." He stood and reached for her hand, pulling her to her feet. "Come on. I hear tell we're on dinner duty tonight."

"Dinner duty? What? You take turns? No one told me!"

He laughed and his arm swung around her, pulling her to him. "We do, my love. That we do. If we're not able to, we make sure there are meals in the freezer."

Chapter 18

Three weeks later, Redmond came looking for his brother, a parcel in hand. He didn't like it. It just had Reilly's name on it, nothing else. He had found it outside the gate on his way home. He paused for a moment to watch Reilly and then approached him.

"Redmond? You're home? I didn't expect you for another day or so." Reilly turned to his brother, a frown coming to his face. "What are you holding?"

"A parcel. A parcel specifically addressed to you. I found it outside the gate." He refused to give it to Reilly. "I'm taking it into the office first. Before you open it."

Reilly watched as Redmond walked away, knowing his brother was right. He turned as he heard footsteps beside him. Aideen stood there, a frown on her face.

"What's with Redmond?"

"He found a parcel outside the gate and is heading back into the office." Reilly turned Aideen around and studied her face. "What can we do that would be fun for you? You're getting stifled here."

"I am, Reilly. I can't handle much more of this, this restriction. I need my freedom." She looked up at him, a closed look on her face.

"Don't even think about running, Aideen."

"I'm not, but I need to get away from here, if only for a few hours. Can we do that?"

The look of pleading on her face broke his heart and he reached to hug her. "Let me talk to Dad and see what we can arrange."

She shoved away from him. "That's part of it, Reilly. You always have to check to make sure it's okay. I can't live like that any more." She turned and ran from him, her steps softened by the carpet on the stairs.

He heard the bedroom door click closed and sighed. He looked up and then ran after her, opening the door to find her standing at the window, staring outside, a defeated slump to her shoulders. He walked to stand behind her, noting that she refused to look at him.

"What would you have me do, Aideen? If we don't take precautions, someone will take you and who knows what will happen."

She finally nodded. When she spoke, her voice was low and tight. "I know, Reilly, I know. I just feel caged."

His hands on her shoulders, he turned her to him, studying her face and then sighed. "All right. Tomorrow, we'll escape for a couple of hours. I just pray I don't regret it."

She nodded, then brushed past him. "Where will we go?"

"Somewhere quiet and simple. I would suggest jeans and sneakers and a sweatshirt."

She turned for a moment and then nodded. "Okay. Reilly, thank you."

"I hope we don't regret it. It's going to be difficult to get away, though."

"I'm sure it will." She paused, wrapping her arms around herself, a shudder running through her.

"I pray we don't regret it." She spun. "Does God really care that much for us, Reilly?"

He nodded, his eyes watchful. "He does, Aideen. He does. He cares for the lowly sparrow. You are worth so much more to Him." And to me, he thought, not putting into words how he felt. It was too soon, he thought. And I may never ever had that chance to tell her that.

The next morning found them leaving early, just as dawn was breaking. He turned away from town, praying no one saw them, and headed for an area he liked to hike in. He needed that time, time with nature, time to commune with God. He prayed that Aideen would find peace there as well. He watched carefully, not seeing anyone around, before he pulled over. No, he thought. I can't go there. Chances are they know that area and will be waiting for us.

Aideen watched for a moment before she spoke. "Is this how far we're going today, Reilly? It's not really that far from your home."

He shook his head. "No. I was heading for somewhere. I don't think we should go there." He tapped the steering wheel with long, tanned fingers. "I have to come up with another plan."

"Can we find a small town to wander through?"

He stared at her. "Just what we can do." He pulled away, heading for a nearby small town, one he didn't think he had been to in years. "We'll try this town. But if I tell you to run, you must."

She nodded, knowing without him putting into words what he meant.

Reilly finally pulled into a parking space, his eyes watchful. He didn't think they had been followed, but he wasn't sure. He had that unsettled feeling that someone was near them that wanted to harm them. He didn't like that. He slid from the car, walking around to open Aideen's door, grasping her hand tight in his.

"Remember, Aideen, if I say run, we run."

She nodded, her eyes on his. "You have a feeling?"

He sighed. "I do. I'm really not sure this was the best idea." He pulled out his phone, checking a text message. "Dad's in touch. I'll let him know where we are and that I'll be in touch every thirty minutes. He's sending one of our team here, just in case. He knows if I miss our check-in time, that something has happened."

She shivered. "Maybe we should just leave, Reilly. I don't like the feeling I'm getting."

He nodded, shutting her door again and then walking around to slide behind the wheel, his fingers idly tapping at the wheel as he sat lost in thought, finally shaking his head and looking at her.

"Where do we go then, Aideen? To keep you safe, I need to take you back to our home. And you're getting stifled there. So am I, to tell you the truth."

Aideen watched him for a moment before she spoke, her words rapid and low. He stared at her before he nodded, reaching for her hand before bowing his head in prayer. She had come up with a plan, but how to do it, he wasn't sure.

He walked around, pulling her from the car, and her hand tight in his, headed for the main street area of the town. They were playing tourist, at least for now. He watched, finally spying the men following them.

"They're here, Reilly?" Aideen had been watching and saw the moment he found the men.

He sighed. "They are. Now, where do we go?"

"We continue to play tourist." She paused at an antique store. "Let's go in here." She pulled him with her, wandering around the store, making her way towards the back door. She glanced around and then, running for the door, was through it and into another store, Reilly on her heels, staring at the store she had entered.

"A clothing store, Aideen?"

She nodded, swiftly sorting through the racks, finding what she wanted and heading for the counter. A few words with the clerk and she was back with him, shoving him towards a change room, handing him clothes. "Here. Quick. Change into this. There's a wig as well. Put it on."

He stared at her, finding her already into another room. He shrugged and then shut the door behind him, changing even as he heard voices at the front of the store. He froze, knowing those voices belonged to the men who were after him. He shoved open the door before he glanced down at what she had chosen. Totally opposite of what he would have. What was her plan?

Aideen peeked out of her change room, nodding to herself that she would not have recognized Reilly, and then pushed her way towards him, her hand catching his and leading him brazenly through the store and out the front door. One of the men held the door for them absentmindedly as he listened to the conversation around him.

Reilly pulled Aideen with him, heading away from the downtown area and towards the edge of town, knowing they would be found if they stayed there. He finally stopped, dropping to a bench.

Aideen sat beside him, her eyes on the way they had come.

"Aideen? Did we really just do that?"

"Just do what?"

"Walk right out by them without them knowing us?" He looked at the outfit she had on, a loose dress, sloppy sandals, a floppy hat and a colourful kerchief tied around her wrist. "How did they not know us?"

She laughed. "We did. Hiding in plain sight, as they say." She pointed to him. "Now, what does your father say?"

He shook his head as he pulled out his phone, then stopped, turning it off. "I don't think I'll answer. We'll find another way of contacting him." He sat, lost in thought, his eyes on her face, watching as she hesitated to speak. "Aideen?"

"I know, Reilly We shouldn't have left today. We shouldn't have run. But I can't sit around any longer. I know your family is looking into things, but this is my life. I need to take back control."

He wrapped an arm around her, not quite sure how to proceed, knowing that he loved her and wanted her with him forever, but that he had promised to set her free when this was over.

Chapter 19

To say Riordan was frustrated was an understatement. He had arisen that morning, early, with news from the office that they were closing in on who was after Aideen. They needed more information from her. He had gone looking for them mid-morning, having finally realized he hadn't seen or heard from them that day. They were nowhere to be found. He sent a text to Reilly, finally hearing that they had needed a day away and that they were safe. He had sent back one, asking that they come home, that he needed to talk with them. Any further attempts had failed, and his calls had gone straight to voice mail.

He turned as Redmond called his name and then hurried towards hm.

"Redmond?"

"They're in Waketown. So are the ones after them. We've lost track of them. Paul saw them head into an antique store and lost them."

Riordan paused and then ran for his vehicle. "He's looking?"

"He is. He hasn't seen them, though. Sam's with him and he can't find them."

Riordan thought through what Redmond said and then began to laugh. "I have a feeling those two walked right by them. Aideen's good. Regan said she told her she could change her appearance and no one would recognize her. I suspect that's what she's done." He paused and then spoke. "Call Paul. Find a clothing store, thrift shop near where they were last seen. Chances are she took Reilly into there, bought some clothes and they walked right out of the store."

Redmond stared at his father. "She wouldn't, would she?" Then he began to shake his head. "Of course, she would. But, how do we find them?"

"I don't think we do. I think they'll find us. I just pray we're in time."

Redmond slipped his phone back into his pocket. "Paul said there was a thrift shop right next door. He saw a couple come out, didn't think anything of it. He's trying to find that couple." He began to laugh. "He doesn't believe you, you know?"

Riordan gave a quick grin. "I'm sure he doesn't. Just pray we reach them in time, that's what we have to do." He found an empty parking spot and slid into it, exiting his vehicle and then locking it. "Where was he heading to look?"

"He was searching downtown as was Sam." Redmond looked around. "I suggest we head to the outskirts."

"I agree. Let's see which one of us find them first."

"Somehow, Dad, I don't think we will."

Reilly watched with interest as his father and brother walked right by them. He could feel Aideen shaking with silent laughter.

"They didn't see us, did they?" Reilly was incredulous at that.

"People see what they want to see. Your Dad and brother are not sure what they're looking for." She looked around. "Now what, Reilly? Do we stay hidden or do we go back to your home?"

He studied her. "I'm not sure. This is not how I planned an escape for you."

"I know." She rose and paced away from him, back towards town, leaving him to run to catch up with her.

"Don't walk away, okay? We need to stay together."

She paused, her face a study of emotions. "But if we're together, we're more apt to be found."

"In these disguises, I hardly think so." He looked down at his ratty jeans, tight T-shirt, and sneakers and then tugged the fedora lower on his head. "These are not how I dress, I will have you know."

She laughed and then pointed. "Let's grab something to eat." She looked around. "There's your Dad. Do you want to speak with him?"

Reilly looked around. "I guess we should somehow. How do you want to?"

She studied Riordan as he paused, staring around. "Let me, okay? I've likely done this more than you." She reached out a hand. "Let me have your car keys."

"What?"

"Your keys. I'm going to give them to him and have Redmond drive it back. We'll go to the other side of town and have your Dad pick us up." She stopped. "No, that won't work." She chewed at her lip.

"You're not thinking straight, Aideen."

She shook her head at him. "No, it's just that if they see us getting into his car, they'll follow him. Who can I call?"

"No one." He grabbed her hand, pulling her with him, back towards the centre of town, finding his car, unlocking it and shoving her in. When he was seated, he turned to her, a stern tone in his voice. "Enough, Aideen. This involves more than you now. It affects my family and our business. We are trying to keep you safe."

She stared at him, before she looked out the window, knowing he was right but unwilling to concede that she needed him in order for her to stay alive. Neither one saw the vehicle approaching them until it went to pass, forcing them off the road.

Aideen screamed as she felt the car hit the shoulder of the road and then continue on through a fence and into a field. She stared at Reilly for a moment before he was around to her door, pulling her from the vehicle and fleeing towards a river, hoping to make it in time. They could heard the shouts of the men behind them.

Reilly finally shoved her down behind some rocks, their breath coming in ragged gasps, a finger to her lips to keep her quiet. He searched the area, finally seeing what he wanted, and pulled her once more with him, shoving her into the shallow cave and pulling the bushes back in front of it. He prayed that the rock path didn't show any scuff marks.

They looked at each other in horror as they heard an explosion rock the air around them and peeking out saw a plume of smoke rising.

"Your car, Reilly! Did they really blow it up?"

He nodded in a grim manner. "They did. They're making sure we don't have transportation. But I know where I can find a vehicle, if we can get to it."

"They'll be searching here soon, won't they?"

He looked up at the sky. "It's getting late. I suspect they'll leave and come back in the morning, if they're city boys and that's what I take them for." He slumped back for a moment, pulling out his phone, staring at it before he slid it back into his pocket.

"You're not calling for help?" Aideen's hand was on his.

"No. I can't be sure they're not tracking that." He looked around and then rose, his hand reaching for hers. "Come on, my love. We need to get moving."

She sighed as she let him pull her to her feet. "I was afraid that's what you would say. Where to?"

Chapter 20

Opening his eyes the following morning, Reilly groaned. Sleeping out in the open, with no protection, was not the piece of cake everyone seemed to think it was. He rose, standing watching Aideen for a moment as she slept, before he looked around, walking to the top of the ridge a few feet away and looking around. They were on the Niagara escarpment, a rocky ridge that ran through the province. He sighed. He had to get her to safety, but there didn't seem to be anywhere that was safe. He turned slightly as he felt something touch his arm.

Aideen stood beside him, a hand up to shade her eyes, before she spoke. "I'm sorry, Reilly. When you suggested a day away, I didn't think we'd end up on the run again." She turned. "Where do we go?"

He pointed down the ridge. "That way. There's a path down there we can follow. We'll find somewhere we can find transportation and new clothes. You need something to eat."

She shook her head, turning it away from him so he couldn't see the tears in her eyes. She finally spoke again. "All right. Lead on."

He took her hand, standing for a moment to pray, asking for protection and guidance. He paused, pulling out his phone, turning it on to send a quick text message, and then turning it off again.

"Won't they track that?" Aideen watched closely.

"No, I don't think they'll have time to do that. I didn't have it on long enough, I don't think." He started down the ridge and realized she hadn't moved. "Aideen?" He turned back, his hand held out. "Come. Now. If you stand up there, you'll be seen."

She finally took his hand, letting him lead her away from there, her eyes watchful, but knowing she was out of her element out in the country. Let her stay in town and she could find places to hide.

They finally stopped at the edge of a small village, Reilly's eyes watchful. He pointed to a bench and they sat. Aideen's head rested against his shoulder for a moment.

"Now what, Reilly?" He could hear the tears in her voice, tears she refused to shed.

"Wait here. I'm just going to go into that store over there and grab some water and food."

She rose. "I'm not staying here on my own."

He sighed. "Please, Aideen?"

She finally agreed, fear running through her, until she say him returning, a backpack on his shoulder. He reached for her hand and led her away, his eyes watching around them. The streets were quiet and he didn't like that. They were too much of a target that way.

Four hours later, he watched as Aideen slumped to the ground in the clearing he had found. She was tired, he knew, and her feet were likely hurting. His were, he thought. He looked around before he dropped down beside her and dug out bottles of water for them both.

She took the bottle, twisting off the cap and sipping before she twisted the cap back on. Her head went down his shoulder and she slept. Reilly watched for a moment, and then he too slept.

Neither one heard the footsteps approaching them or saw the four men, dressed in matching Polo shirts and jeans. The four men studied them and then nodded to one another. One reached to scoop Aideen into his arms before two others helped Reilly to his feet.

Reilly shook his head, groggy with sleep, not fully awake as his arm was draped over one of the men's shoulder and walked away from there. They were stuffed into a van and the van left. Thirty minutes after the van drove away, three men ran from the pathway looking around, not seeing them. Curses, loud words, and accusations flew among them before they headed away from there. Their boss would not be happy, they knew. How had the two disappeared?

Reilly finally roused, his eyes darting around the room, and he sprang to his feet, dropping back to the bed as his head spun. He rose slowly again and searched the room, a frown on his face. Reaching for the door, he was surprised to see it open. This is strange, he thought, as he walked out into the hall. Where is Aideen, he wondered?

He paused at a room door, seeing it open, and looked in, walking towards the bed and sinking down to sit beside Aideen. She was asleep, he could tell, seeing the dark circles under her eyes and the fatigue on her face. He studied her, knowing he had to take her home, but how he wasn't sure.

He heard footsteps stop in the doorway behind him and drew a deep breath, finally rising and walking towards the older man standing watching him. He walked towards the room he was pointed to, finding a kitchen. He sat at the table, surprised to find coffee and a meal waiting for him.

"Eat." The man spoke. "Eat, Reilly, and then we talk."

Reilly shot him a look, a frown in place. "Do I know you?"

"We haven't seen each other since you were small. Your Dad called me."

"Dad? Is he here?" Reilly went to stand, but a hand on his shoulder kept him in his chair.

"No, he's not. We'll talk. First, get some food into you." The man paused, his eyes tracing towards the doorway. "We've got some fluid down your wife. She's sleeping again. She's a feisty one, isn't she?"

Reilly's hand paused as he lifted his mug to his mouth. "Feisty? What did she do?"

"She told us off, tried to walk away, and then ate. She's been through a lot, I would say."

"She has, more than anyone should have to." Reilly studied his plate and pushed it away, his appetite gone. "So, talk. Tell me where we are and who you are."

The man reached for the coffee pot, refilling Reilly's mug and then his own before he sat, a thumb running up and down the handle of his mug. He watched Reilly closely, seeing in him characteristics and looks of an old friend.

"Your Dad and I went to school together. We went our separate ways when you were small, Reilly. We started up the business we're in together, but realized that we each wanted to go about it a separate way." He sipped at his coffee. "I'm Matthew Sedore."

Reilly stared at him. "Matthew? Dad talks about you a lot. I didn't know he had kept in touch."

Matthew shook his head. "He hasn't. Not really. We send cards at Christmas, but other than that, we don't have contact, which is a good thing.

People would have to really dig to find a connection between us. Somehow, I don't think the ones after you have the brains to do that."

"But, they'll find us. That takes smarts."

Matthew shook his head. "Not really. They find your vehicle and track it. That's what they've been doing. I hear they blew your vehicle up."

"That's what we thought. I can't imagine how Dad felt."

"It scared him, Reilly. It scared him enough that he contacted me. He asked if we can help you."

Reilly stared at him. "But what do you do? How can you help?"

"I'm into security, Reilly. I protect people. That's what we've been asked to do." He paused, taking a sip of his coffee. "My men followed you yesterday. You were both sleeping when they found you. I know that's not you. That's not how you work. You're exhausted, you're worried, and you're not thinking straight. We get that. If we hadn't found you, they would have. We have word they were less than an hour behind us."

Reilly shook his head. "I know, Matthew. I know. It's just……"

Matthew smiled. "I know, son. I've been there. Young and in love."

"The thing of it is, Matthew, is that even though I love her, I promised to set her free once she's out of danger. That was a bargain we made."

Matthew nodded "I see. Then you have your work cut out for you." He rose, pacing. "Now, we have to keep you two safe for now. Your Dad's been in touch, but we're keeping it to a minimum. Just for your safety." He excused himself before he walked back in.

"Matthew?" Reilly was watching him, knowing something was up.

"Your brother contacted us. Whoever it is after you two tried to break into your property. They caught them, but can't get them to talk."

Reilly nodded, then turned his head before he rose as he heard Aideen's voice. He stopped in her doorway, finding her spinning in a circle, panic in her very voice.

"Aideen?"

His voice stopped her and she turned to him, before running to him to be enveloped in his arms. He felts the shudders running through her, knowing she was trying hard not to weep.

He stood, his head on hers, for how long he never knew afterwards before she looked up at him.

"Where are we? I was so afraid when I didn't see you."

"We're with friends. They found us yesterday and brought us here." He searched her face before he turned her towards the doorway. "Come. They have food for us. Hungry?"

She shook her head. "No, not really. I could use a tea, though."

He seated her, turning to the counter, finding Matthew handing him a cup of tea. He nodded, searching Matthew's face.

"Here you go, my love. Matthew has a tea already for you." He set it before her before he sat beside her, his hand reaching for her.

She looked up at Matthew, a frown on her face, before it left. "I know you."

"You do, Aideen. We were involved with your security before you ran." He pointed at her. "You caused a lot of consternation, you know."

She sighed. "I know. It's just I had no idea who I could trust."

"We get that. This time, you're not running. We're keeping you under lock and key. I mean that literally, Aideen. You and Reilly are now in our care and custody." He shook his head at her as she went to speak. "No, not this time, Aideen. This time, we do it our way. You're not running. You put a lot of people at risk by doing just that."

She finally sat back, her eyes on him, a closed look on her face. "I don't like it."

"We don't care if you don't like it or not. It's what will keep you and Reilly alive. Stop and think about that one. How long will Reilly live if they catch him?"

She spun in her chair, her eyes on Reilly, who was watching her closely, no emotions on his face at all. "Then, he'll just have to leave."

"It doesn't work that way, Aideen. Not any more. You two have been seen together. They'll assume you mean something to one another and take him to flush you out. So for now, you're together." Matthew finally rose, walking away, his phone in his hand, needing to make a call, one he had never thought he would need to make.

"Aideen, he's right, you know. We have to stay here." Reilly's hand reached to stop hers from moving on the tabletop. "We have to trust him."

"Do you? Do you trust him?"

Reilly shrugged. "I know Dad did, at some point. He says he's an old friend of Dad's." He pulled out his phone, sent off a quick text and waited for a response. His father was quick to reply, stating they should stay where they were for now. He was working on a solution. Reilly shut off his phone and pocketed it. "For now, Dad says to stay here."

"Reilly, we need to talk, somewhere we can't be overheard. There's something wrong about all this." Aideen pulled him to his feet and then through the outside door, searching for a place they could talk without being overheard.

"Aideen? What are you talking about?"

"Reilly, they were my security before I ran, but someone kept getting through to me. I would have notes, cards, packages left. Threats. I talked to Matthew and he couldn't find the leak. I think it's one of his men or else him. That's why I took off. I don't trust him."

Reilly turned her so he could watch the house behind her. "Are you sure?"

She nodded, her eyes on his face, willing him to trust her. "How well does your father know him now?"

Reilly shrugged. "I don't remember him at all. Dad has spoken of him over the years, but I sense a hesitation in his voice." He groaned. "We could be in his hands, waiting for him to turn us over to whoever it is after you." He spun as he heard yells from the front of the house and saw Matthew running towards them before he fell.

Reilly grabbed for her hand and ran, searching for a hiding place. "In here." He shoved her into a small barn and then up to the loft, down behind piles of hay bales. His arm held her tight, his finger on her mouth.

They heard the doors open and then footsteps moving around, before they heard someone climb the ladder and look around. They waited, finally hearing the footsteps leave and the door creak closed.

They waited, hearing the door open again and cautious footsteps walking around below them, before they heard low voices.

"They're not in here. Where are they? I thought you said they ran this way."

"They did. I've looked, even up there. They're not here."

"They have to be around here somewhere. Our contact said they were." Anger laced the voice. "He's not going to be very pleased if we don't bring them back with us."

"If we can't find them, we can't, can we?"

They heard a small pop and then only one set of footsteps walking away. Aideen stared at Reilly, her eyes huge. He just shook his head, before he lowered it, trying to think how they could get away. Hours passed, before he finally looked around, pointing to the small window behind them. She nodded and rose, walking over to it. She looked down, her heart in her throat before she turned back to him.

"There's no way we can get down there, Reilly." Her voice was a whisper.

He looked down and groaned, a grim look on his face. "We'll have to go down then, my love. Here, I'll go first."

Their feet had barely hit the dirt floor when the door opened. Reilly spun, shoving Aideen behind them, his fists up ready to fight before he lowered them.

“Redmond?”

He nodded, his hand beckoning them out and towards the back of the property, not saying a word. Reilly headed that way, Aideen’s hand tight in his. He watched carefully, not seeing anyone else around.

Finally, safe in a vehicle, he spoke.

“Redmond? What’s going on?”

Redmond stared at him and then at Aideen. “It’s a good thing you two took off when you did.”

“What are you talking about?”

“We’ve had to go into hiding, all of us.” Redmond watched as Aideen’s eyes slid closed. “They tried to get into our house, Reilly. So far, not one of our family has been hurt. They were waiting for Dad and I when we got home yesterday. Was it only yesterday?”

“Rory and Leah?”

“They’re safe. So are Mom and the girls. They’re at our office complex.” He turned back to the road and then started the vehicle. “We found your car. They are ramping up their search. What did you get mixed up in, Aideen?”

She shook her head. “I have no idea, Redmond. All I did was give the authorities the paperwork Adam left. That’s all. I had no idea what all he was involved in.” She shuddered, fear running through her. “Now where?”

“Now where? We need to find a place to keep you safe.” He shared a look with Reilly.

“Matthew?”

“One of his men was a contact for them. Matthew didn’t make it. I’m sorry, Reilly. He tried to protect you. The police have arrested that man and one other, but they're still working the scene."

"The man in the barn?"

"Him? That was one of the men after you, I suspect."

Chapter 21

Reilly paced his office, his eyes on Aideen as she sat huddled down on the couch, a blanket covering her, her eyes closed. He thought she was sleeping but he wasn't sure of anything about her any more. He turned as the door opened and his father beckoned him out.

"Reilly? You're okay?"

"I am, Dad, just frustrated, worried, what have you."

Riordan gave a grim nod. "I know. I know why you took off yesterday. What happened would have happened at some point." He ran his hand along his chin. "Matthew was dirty, Reilly. I didn't know that. I would not have thought that."

Reilly stared at him, shock on his face. "He was?"

"That's right. I would not have sent you there if I had known. So far, from what the police have said, he's the only one. His men were clean." Sorrow briefly crossed his face. "I'm sorry, Reilly. I sent you to him, thinking to keep you safe."

"I know, Dad. Whoever is after Aideen has far reaching tentacles, don't they?" He turned to look through the door. "Now what?"

"Now what? That's a good question. I'm working with the investigators now. They have asked if we can keep her with us for now. They may want to move her to protective custody and hide her away somewhere."

"Not happening, Dad.   She's not going anywhere without me."

"That's what I told them. They are not happy with you two."

Reilly gave a grim smile. "I doubt they would be. Now, what do we do?"

"We keep searching. Somewhere, there's an answer. I've pulled as many of our people as I can to work on this." Riordan paused, his hand on his son's shoulder as he prayed for him, silently, even as his mind sorted through the information he had. "Has she said anything else?"

Reilly shook his head. "She's at a loss, Dad. She has nothing of Adam's or her parents. She has no idea who he was working for." He turned as he heard a sound and walked back into the office, reaching for Aideen as she ran for him, his arms tight around her. "Aideen?"

"Oh, Reilly! What did I do?" She burrowed her head against him as she wrapped her arms around him. "I remember."

"What do you remember?" Reilly tried to set her back from him but couldn't. "Aideen? What did you remember?"

"A name." When she murmured it, Reilly's eyes flew to his father's. Riordan's face grew grimmer, if that was possible, and he walked away. He had more research to do, and he knew the name.

Reilly finally managed to get Aideen to look up at him before he sighed, drawing her down on the couch, his arm around her.

"How is he connected to Adam?"

"He's an uncle on our mother's side. I didn't connect them until now. Something you said earlier made me think of that." Aideen stared ahead of her. "Reilly, how do we do this? I don't want you hurt."

"We're taking every precaution we can. Dad's running the name now. He'll pass it on to the police, I suspect, at some point."

She snorted. "That won't work. He's likely ahead of us."

Reilly looked up as he heard his father's voice and then Riordan entered his office, shutting the door, and finding a chair he pulled over and sat, his eyes on the younger couple.

"Dad? What did you find?"

Riordan shook his head. "That name? Aideen, he's dead, has been for years. Why would you mention him?"

She stared at him. "No, he's not. He showed up with Adam at my door about six months ago. What's going on?" She turned to Reilly. "You believe me, don't you?"

"I do. Dad?"

"I do, Reilly." He held up a hand as Aideen went to speak. "Redmond and Rory are working through a search for us. They hope to have more information soon." He searched their faces. "Right now, we need to figure out what's going on." He pointed to the door. "We'll move to the conference room, Reilly. We have all the information so far. I need Aideen to help us work through it."

Two days later, Reilly stared around the room, seeing progress being made but knowing they had a long way to go. He reached for Aideen, pulling her with him and outside to a sheltered yard.

"We're not safe out here, Reilly." She tried to pull her hand free.

"Just for five minutes, Aideen. You need a break. You haven't left that room in two days."

"No, I haven't. I want this over. You need to be free to go on with your life and you're not able to do that. Not until I'm in no danger." She refused to look at him, her eyes raised to the sky, as she stood, arms wrapped around herself.

He sighed, knowing that sooner or later, he'd have to talk to her, to let her know he didn't want to let her go, ever. But that couldn't happen. Not yet. He turned as he heard the door and his father emerged, his eyes on his son.

"Reilly?"

"She needed air. Dad."

"I see. When you two come back in, find me. I'll be in my office." He turned, hesitating and then walking back inside.

"What did he want, Reilly?"

Reilly sighed, hearing the apprehension, fear and anger in her voice. "I don't know. He didn't say." He reached for her hand, tugging her with him and back inside. "He said he wanted to talk to us."

He shoved her down in a chair in his father's office and stood her, ready to keep her in her chair, even as he studied his father. Something had happened, and I don't think we're going to like it.

"Aideen? The police have been in touch. The investigation is moving ahead but they want to put you into protective custody."

"Not happening, Riordan. Absolutely not. I had that all my life. I just can't. It would kill me."

"And it will kill you if they don't." Riordan studied her, seeing that she was at her breaking point. "I've told them that, but they still want to do that. In fact, they will be here this afternoon. I can't put them off any longer." He looked up at Reilly. "They won't take you with her, Reilly. I'm sorry."

Reilly nodded, having expected that. "I see, Dad. I need to talk to Aideen. Excuse us."

Aideen turned to Reilly as he paced the bedroom. "Reilly, I can't do this."

"I know you can't. I'm not ready to let you go into custody. They'll find you, I know that." He paused, a look crossing his face, before he was at the closet, pulling out backpacks and throwing one at her. "Here. Pack clothes that you would need if you were camping." She paused, staring at him. "Do it, Aideen. We're leaving before they get here. We're going on the run again."

"Reilly! We can't!"

"We can. We have no choice. Hurry. I want to be out of here in thirty minutes. Dad will stall for us."

"He will? He doesn't know what we're doing."

"He'll know. He understands." Reilly dug out his wallet, checking for cash, before he headed for his office and swung open a safe, pulling out cash and sticking it into his pocket. He held out some for her. "Here, stick this into your pockets. We may need it."

He grabbed her hand and pulled her with him, not out the front door as she suspected, but to the back door and the garage. He pointed to a motorcycle and then dropped their backpacks in the storage compartments before handing her a helmet.

"On you get, Aideen. This is mine. No one other than family know I have it, I hope. We're off." With that, he was out of the back door of the garage, the motorcycle heading for the back gate, that swung open as he approached it and then closed behind them. They were once more on the run, on their own, with no support.

Aideen clutched him around the waist, her head buried against him as much as she could, not liking that they were on the run, but knowing she would do that rather than go into custody somewhere and lose what little freedom she had.

Chapter 22

Finally stopping at a campground, Reilly swung his leg over the bike and turned to Aideen, a smile on his face. She was glaring at him.

"Just where are we?"

"At a little known campground. They rent tents and equipment here. We just need to get some supplies." He pointed to the bike. "Stay here. I'll be right back."

He was back in short order, pushing the bike towards a campsite. "This is ours. It's the only one left. God prepared it for us."

"I don't get it, Reilly. How?"

"It had been rented. I researched campground near home, knowing we would likely have to run again. This one seemed the best suited. I wasn't sure if there would be an empty spot, but I prayed there would be."

"Does He really do that?"

Reilly nodded. "He does and will. I have had to learn to trust Him in a way that most people don't." He touched her cheek, wanting to make it all better for her but knowing that wouldn't be possible.

She shook her head, even as she stooped to peer into the tent. "There are no sleeping bags, Reilly."

"I know."

She spun at the tone in his voice, her eyes narrowed. "Just what are you up to?"

He wrapped her into his arms, a whisper in her ear and then she nodded before she stepped back. "So, where do we go for supplies?"

"There's a town near here. We can go there." He handed her the helmet she had worn. "Let's see what we can find."

He made a point of stopping at the office, letting the manager know they were heading into town but would be back within two hours. He sat on his bike for a moment before he headed off, not towards town, but in another direction.

Hours later, he quietly pushed the bike towards a cottage, Aideen following with her hand on his back. He stopped, looking around, and then nodded towards the house. She ran for it even as he headed for the detached garage and opening it, stashed the bike, grabbing their packs and the supplies they had finally stopped to purchase. He looked around as he shut the door and then ran for the cottage.

Aideen watched as he searched for the key, finding it and opening the door, waiting for her to walk through before he shut and locked the door behind him. He dropped his burdens and reached for her, drawing her into a tight hug before he stood back, hands on her arms.

"We should be okay here for a few days. No one knows about this cottage."

"They don't? How? Or should I say who?"

"A friend, one I don't contact unless I need to. There is no connection that anyone would ever find between us." He picked up her backpack and headed for one of the bedrooms. "You can use this one, if you wish, or take your pick. The bathroom is down the hall there. I suspect you want to get cleaned up."

Aideen stood in the bedroom, her eyes on the door closing behind her, before she looked around. Rugged. Rustic. Comfortable. She was at a loss to describe it, she thought. She shrugged, reaching for her pack and clean cloths. She rushed through a shower, wanting to leave hot water for Reilly. Wrapping a towel around her wet hair, she padded on bare feet towards the kitchen, hearing the kettle whistling and smiling. A cup of tea would be welcome.

Reilly stood for a moment in the doorway, watching as Aideen worked away in the kitchen, his thoughts dark before he turned for a shower himself. He stood once more when he was done, watching her as she sat at the table, twisting her mug in her hands. He walked towards her, a hand running over her shoulders, before he reached for the pot of coffee.

"Are you hungry?" He turned when she didn't speak, finding her asleep in just those few moments. He sighed, and then gathered her close and carried her to her bed, covering her, a hand resting on her hair as he prayed for her. It would be a long time before he sought his own sleep and that would be on the worn couch in the living room, where he could keep watch.

Aideen stirred in the early morning hours, listening to the sounds of nature stirring outside her window, the sounds of the soft rain as it hit the tin roof, and opened her eyes, feeling safe for the first time in months, she thought. She laid there, her thoughts drifting before she rose, a puzzled look on her face. She had no memories of going to bed and just why was she still in the clothes she had changed to the night before. Opening the door as quietly as she could, she stood, her eyes on Reilly as he slept, one arm tucked under his head, the other arm across his chest.

She walked towards him, her feet silent on the worn floor before she headed for the kitchen, seeing that he had cleaned up the night before. She sighed. She had not met a family like his, she thought, who put others first like they did. Then, she snorted. She hadn't met too many families at that. Her parents had made sure of that. Her hand reached for the kettle and then for the coffee pot, making the coffee for him that she knew he enjoyed. She turned to the fridge, opening it and pulling out supplies. How did so much fresh food get there? They hadn't shopped for that much, she knew.

She turned speculative eyes towards the doorway and then nodded. His friend, that's who. Bless him, whoever it is.

Reilly roused, the smell of coffee tickling at his nose. He frowned as his eyes opened and he shot up on the couch, before he relaxed. Aideen must be up, he thought, and rose, stopping in the doorway to watch as she worked away. Lord, please, protect my lady. If it is Your will, let her be willing to be my lady for the rest of our lives. I don't know if I can stand to let her go, but I will if I must.

Reilly walked towards Aideen, his hand running down her hair before he reached for a mug and poured his coffee, moving away to stand at the outside door, staring at the rain. Thank you, Lord. You sent rain to cover our tracks. This cottage is isolated, but I'm not sure if it's isolated enough. Seth said he had stocked up for us, but to let him know if we needed anything. Who would have thought that a name from the past would have come to me? But that was You, wasn't it, Lord? Whatever happened to us in the past, that day we saved each other when we were rock climbing, it cemented a friendship and a way to keep my lady safe.

Aideen spoke from beside him and he reached to wrap an arm around him.

"What was that, my love?"

"Are we safe here, Reilly? At least for a bit?" Worry underlined her words.

"I think we are. No one should know about this friend. We haven't spoken in years, until God brought his name to my mind yesterday."

She nodded, finally looking towards the table. "I have breakfast ready, if you want to eat."

"I do. Thank you." He dropped a kiss on her hair, before he swung her around and then seated her at the table, reaching for her hands as he sat, asking a blessing on their food.

Aideen finally reached for her mug of tea, sipping at it as she watched him. "What do we do now, Reilly?" She sighed. "I guess that's our theme song."

"What is?" He watched her, a smile on his face, not knowing that his love for her shone in his eyes.

She studied him, not sure what she was reading on his face. "Our theme song. What do we do now."

He grinned. "I guess that would be it. For now, we relax. We rest. We talk. We pray. We wait." His grin widened at the look on her face. "Dad said he would be in touch. I have a secure email I can check in a couple of days. He knew we'd run. He'll cover for us. I didn't tell him for sure what I was planning. That way he can he has no idea what we're up to."

"Will that get him into trouble?"

Reilly shrugged. "He's not worried about that. He knows the police won't be happy, but he couldn't stop you if you decided to leave. That's a given. You were not under arrest."

"Not yet." She sighed. "So how do we do this, Reilly?"

Chapter 23

Aideen was on a hunt two days later. She needed to talk to Reilly and could not find him in the cottage. She stood on the back deck, looking around, finally seeing him walking back towards her.

"Reilly?"

"Aideen. Sorry. I just wanted to take a look at the lake. If you're up to it, we can go out in the canoe tonight. We should be safe."

"Oh, that would be wonderful. I've always wanted to do that." She stood, watching his face, seeing him relaxing over the last few days. "Have you heard from your father?"

"I haven't checked my email yet. Let's go do that." He reached for her hand, liking how it fit into his.

Aideen waited as Reilly accessed his email, a frown on his face as he read it before he abruptly shut down his phone. She reached for his hand.

"Reilly?"

"The police never showed that afternoon. Dad has been in contact with the top investigator. They never planned on being there. Someone close to the investigation is playing us." He looked at her. "Dad says for us to stay where we are for now. If he has to, he'll find us. Right now, he is frantically working to find who is responsible for the leaks."

Aideen looked at him, sorrow on her face. "It will be one of your men, I think, Reilly. One of your men has been gotten to. That's how this man works."

Reilly nodded. "Dad's aware of that and he and Rory are working through that. It hurts that someone you've trusted your life to does this."

"It does. I have never had that kind of trust before." She bit at her lip, not sure how to proceed. "Have they come up with any more names or information?"

"Dad didn't say, kept the email short. I get that he had to, but we're not going to be prepared if we don't know."

"That's why we stay here. Your friend, will he come here?"

Reilly shook his head. "He hardly ever comes here. Once every couple of months, and that for only a few hours. He bought this a few years ago, as a retirement home, he said. At least, that was his plan."

Aideen finally rose, heading for the bookshelves, trying to find something that would catch her attention. She studied the photos, a frown on her face, before she gave an exclamation and turned to the doorway where Reilly stood watching her.

"Aideen?" Reilly walked towards her. "What's wrong?"

"Your friend? What does he do?"

Reilly shrugged. "He's in law enforcement. Why?"

She pointed to a photo. "Is that him?"

Reilly nodded, a puzzled look on his face. "It is. Why?"

"Because we need to leave. He's one of the ones that I saw with Adam."

"What?" Reilly took a look at her and then shoved her towards her bedroom. "Pack. Now."

He had them on the bike and out of there in short order, missing the men who ran towards the cottage, spreading out to search, standing in consternation and anger that they weren't there.

Reilly finally pulled over, his phone out as he contacted his father, listening to his quick words before he pocketed his phone and took off again. Aideen clung to him, not sure what was happening.

Finally able to get of the bike, Aideen spun on Reilly, her mouth open to speak. The words died on her lips as she watched him.

"Reilly?"

He looked up, a bleak look on his face. "They found us, Aideen. You were right. He was one of them."

"Where do we go then, Reilly? Do we have to leave the province?"

He shook his head. "Dad's working on a plan. I can't do this, Aideen. I can't keep running with you. It won't work."

"I know it won't. I've tried it for so many years and it never worked for me." She paced, her eyes on the sky. "So, what do we do?"

"We head home, I guess. I have no idea where we can go that they won't find us." Reilly watched as she paused, before she turned to him. "No more games, Aideen. We don't have time for that. Dad said the trial is upcoming, in the next week or two. The prosecutor wants to talk to you."

She shook her head. "That was not part of my deal. My deal with them was for Adam. I refused to help them with any other."

"They know that, but given what's going on, they want you in." He paused as she shook her head. "What? What did you just think about?"

"I don't think this is related to Adam. Not directly. If he's dead, why keep going after me? I don't understand that."

"That's what we don't get. You're not a danger to him now. So, who is after you?" Reilly paced, a sudden thought clenching at his heart. "Aideen, did any of his friends show interest in you?"

"What do you mean?" She stared at him and then paled, her head shaking. "No. No. It can't be."

He reached for her, supporting her as her legs gave way. "What did you remember?"

"Not one of his friends. One of Dad's. He used to watch me all the time. I got so I kept out of the way as much as I could. I didn't like the way he looked at me." She looked at him, horror on her face. "Is it him?"

"Let me have his name and I'll get Dad to look into it." He pocketed his phone when he was finished, his eyes on Aideen, a heavy burden on his heart. His father had confirmed her thoughts, but let him know that the man was in hospital, not expected to live.

Aideen shuddered as she said the name, not seeing Reilly pause, sending a look at her, his heart dropping. He knew the man, they had been after him for years, unable to prove anything against him. He also knew the police were after him.

He finally reached and tucked her back onto the bike and straddled it, his hands on the handlebars, not sure where to head any more. She spoke softly in his ear as he turned his head to listen, and he nodded.

Chapter 24

Riordan looked up from his notes, standing as he saw Reilly in the doorway, Aideen beside him. He walked towards them, hesitating and then reaching to hug first Reilly and then Aideen before he motioned them in and shut the door.

"Did anyone see you?"

"Just Rory and Ryanne. They got us in here." Reilly paced, finally stopping in front of where Aideen sat. He nodded at the look on her face. "Dad, where do we stand?"

"We found our leak it. It was George Peterson."

Reilly nodded. "I'm not surprised. He never really fit."

"He didn't. Now, what do we do with you two?"

"We need to come up with a plan, but we want to go on the offensive. Aideen is refusing to hide anymore and I can't say that I blame her. Even hidden, she's getting found."

Riordan sank down on the edge of his desk, waiting, watching, knowing the two had come up with a plan. "So, what is your plan?"

"We're going to start living a live that most people do. We're not hiding anymore. We're going to be seen out and about. Go for dinners, drives, walk the beaches. Whatever it is." Reilly stared at his father. "I know, Dad. I know. You're worried. And you have every right to worry." Reilly turned to watch Aideen. "We want to go house hunting as well, Dad. Isn't that what newlyweds do?"

"They do. Are you sure?" Riordan's heart had sank as he heard their plans, knowing it would be impossible to keep them safe.

"We are, Dad. They're out there, watching. The longer it goes on the more dangerous it is for everyone involved." He turned to face his father. "I'll need to find a vehicle."

"Use one of the business ones for now." Riordan and Reilly shared a long look before Reilly nodded.

Reilly turned to Aideen, finding her drooping where she sat. "I need to get Aideen somewhere she can sleep."

"The apartment here. Your mother has had it cleaned and stocked. We didn't know which one of us would be using it. Take her there for now."

Reilly reached for Aideen's hand and helped her to her feet, leading her away from his father, not knowing when or where he would see him again. With the plans they had made, they had decided not to have a lot of contact with his family, just to keep them as safe as they could.

Riordan sighed and then looked up as Naomi stood in the hallway, watching the younger couple before she entered, a frown on her face.

"Wasn't that Reilly?"

"It was. They're back, sort of." Riordan stood, pacing.

"What do you mean, sort of? Either they are or they aren't?"

"They're here for today. They plan on going on the offensive, putting themselves out there. Reilly said they tried running and hiding and that didn't work." Riordan stopped and turned watching his wife, seeing the distress on her face.

"Not that. They can't."

"We can't stop them. We need to work with them. I'll talk to Reilly later tonight. Right now, they need some time to rest. He didn't say but I can tell this has taken a lot from them."

"Oh, love, what can we do? Other than pray." Naomi walked into her husband's arms, feeling the strength there she needed.

"Other than that, not a whole lot. I'll have someone watch them. Reilly knows that is a given. He's accepted that. Aideen on the other hand not likely will. She's a stubborn lady."

"She is and we need to end this, Riordan. They can't go on with their lives until it is."

Riordan sighed, his eyes on the doorway. "You know once it is, Reilly will set her free, let her walk away from him."

"He can't. She's meant for him."

"It will have to be her choice, love, not ours. Not Reilly's. You know that was the bargain he made with."

"I know, but I can still pray they stay together."

Riordan gave a low laugh. "And I know you will do just that."

Aideen looked around the apartment, feeling at home and not sure why. "Who decorated this?"

"Decorated? I think Mom had originally. Then Rory's Leah walked in and redid it. Mom let her. Why?"

"It's comfortable. What does she do again?"

"She has a B&B. Rory works from there. Why?"

"Can we go there? Would it be safe?"

Reilly stared at her, a thought coming to his mind. "It should be. Let's stay here for a day or so, make our plans, and then go from there. You're exhausted, Aideen. And to tell you the truth, so am I. We need to regain our strength. This is coming up to the end game."

"I know, Reilly.' She paced, finally reaching for her backpack and heading the bedroom area, studying them and choosing one, the door clicking closed behind her.

Reilly blew out a breath, his head dropping down for a moment before he too grabbed his pack and headed for the adjacent bedroom. Showered, shaved, in clean clothes, he returned to the kitchen, making his coffee and her tea and then reaching into the fridge for food. He paused as he heard her footsteps behind him and she reached for her mug before heading back into the living room area. He shook his head. No, now was not the time he wanted to speak with her about what his father had just told him, but he had no choice.

Aideen stood for a moment, staring out the window, sipping at her tea before she looked down at her mug. Reilly remembered what she liked, she thought, and turned, a speculative look on her face. He was becoming important to her, but she kept her feelings hidden. She could not move on with anything, not with this hanging over her. She reached for the plate of sandwiches he held out, moving to set them on the coffee table, sitting herself and finding her hand nestled into his as he prayed. She would miss this, she thought. She blinked back the tears, knowing what she had to do.

Reilly watched her closely, knowing she was trying to come up with a plan to get away and keep him safe.

"Don't, Aiden." When she looked at him, he spoke again. "Don't run. If you do, take me with you. Let us make a stand. If he's done this to you, who else has he done it to?"

She turned to him, a startled look on her face, and she set her sandwich back down. "That's what has been bothering me, Reilly. Why me? Who else, as you say?"

Reilly pulled out his phone, his finger in the air, and called Riordan, asking him to research that. Riordan's voice was startled and then grim.

An hour later, Reilly walked to the door, a quiet tap startling Aideen. He opened it to find Redmond and Regan there. He stepped back, watching them both closely.

"What did you find?"

"Enough that we can go to the police with our investigation." Redmond paced towards Aideen, who sat watching him. "Aideen, what made you think of that?"

"It wasn't me. It was him." She pointed to Reilly. "He's the one who said that. Why?"

Regan handed over a photo. "This is why."

Aideen took the photo, not looking at it, her eyes on Reilly, before she looked down, a small cry torn from her. "Who is this?"

"That's what we're working on. The police are as well." Regan gently took the picture back and handed it to Reilly.

"This looks so much like you, Aideen, but it's not you. Who is it?"

"That's what we have to confirm, but the police think it is a relation of yours, Aideen. Who would she be?"

"I have no idea. I never knew of any female relations." She looked up. "Is she the one they're after?"

"That's what we think. Not you. Somehow they found you and either think you're her or that you can lead them her."

Aideen shivered. "I don't know her. Why me?"

Reilly gave a muffled sound and was at her side, his arms around her, holding her as she wept and then scooping her into his arms as she slept, carrying her to her rest, Regan ahead of him to pull down the covers for him. He stood, his eyes hooded as he watched her, before he turned, walking back to where his siblings waited, watching as Redmond pocketed his phone.

"Redmond?"

"She's not related to her, just looks like her. We have confirmation that she's the one the man is after. Not Aideen. All this with her has been a mistake, a huge mistake."

Reilly was shaking his head. "No, it's not. Someone is after her. Is Dad or the police putting out a statement?"

Regan nodded, looking up from a text message. "Dad says the police will release a statement tomorrow. But that won't keep your lady safe, Reilly. We still need to find them."

"I know, and I have no idea how to do just that." He looked up at a sound from Regan. "Regan? You have a plan. We planned to become more visible, but I'd like to hear yours."

They spoke, discussed, argued and finally came to a consensus, Aideen walking back in on the tail end of the discussion.

Chapter 25

Staring up at the house before her, Aideen's mouth dropped open, until a tap of Reilly's finger closed it. She glared at him for a moment.

"It's beautiful. And it's Leah's?"

"It is. It was her family home. She turned it into a bed and breakfast to make ends meet. Someday, she or Rory will need to tell you their adventure. And before you asked, I was part of it. Leah and I disappeared for a while."

"You did? I hope that doesn't happen again. Will we be safe here, Reilly? Will we bring trouble to them?"

He shrugged. "It won't make any difference where we go. Until they find your lookalike and the men after her, we are in danger. And don't say it. Rory and Leah are well aware of what they're facing and are willing to put themselves out there for us." He reached for her hand, leading her into the house and then into the private quarters, not seeing the speculative looks sent their way.

Rory stood from the table he had been sitting at, coming first to hug Reilly and then stood, his eyes assessing Aideen as she looked around before she looked up at him, a shuttered look on her face. Rory sighed to himself. Here we go again, Lord. Reilly's turn.

Aideen finally turned, heading for the back door, seeing Leah out there and needing to talk to a female. Leah turned as she heard the door, a smile on her face as she reached to hug Aideen before she drew her down the yard to a seat.

Reilly watched Aideen walk away and then turned to Rory. "Has Dad called?"

"He has. I was waiting for you to show up. He said you likely would." He pointed at a chair. "Sit. This is going to take time."

"This sounds ominous."

"It's not. Dad said they found the lady, who really doesn't look like Aideen. They suspect her photo was doctored that way."

"She doesn't?" Reilly drew a deep breath. "So, it was a plant, like we thought."

"It was. It means that whoever it is out there is still looking for your lady." He held up a hand as Reilly went to speak. "We're fine with you two here. Leah has been working on the old shed at the back and has turned it into a really nice guest suite. No one has rented it yet. She has refused, until now. She wants you and Aideen to use it. It's close to the house, but separate enough that if something happens, you two can get away."

"That's good. Somehow, I think we'll need that." Reilly paused. "There's still something I don't understand. Were they her parents?"

Rory nodded. "They were. From what we have determined, they never wanted her. Her mother resented having her. Her father had hoped to have another son but with a daughter, he turned his back on her. Her brother always had a sadistic streak, hidden from most, but he took it out on Aideen, picking up on how her parents felt about her."

"The woman she remembers?"

"That was a nanny they hired. She died from heart disease about the time Aideen says she disappeared."

Reilly nodded, his head turning as he heard the ladies' voices. Leah came to hug him and then stood, her hand on his shoulder, her eyes on Rory, before she spoke.

"I showed Aideen the cottage. She loves it. She said she wanted to live there permanently."

"Is that so?" Rory grinned at Aideen. "We can arrange that, you know. I know Reilly has been restless at work. Maybe it's time he found a new line of work."

Reilly shook his head at him as he rose. "Aideen, would you show me the cottage, if that's all right with Leah?"

She took his hand, leading him from the kitchen, leaving the couple remaining staring after them, hearts raised in prayer for them.

"It's cute, but homey, Reilly. Just what I have always dreamed of." She stood in the doorway, watching as he walked through before he came back and drew her inside and into his arms. She felt like she had come home but knew it was an illusion. Soon, she would be on her way.

Reilly turned in a circle, taking her with him as he did so. "I like this. You're right. It feels like home." He rested his chin on her hair. "We need to talk, Aideen."

"I know but we need this over more." She moved away from him, her heart sick at the thought he wanted his freedom. How, Lord, do I let him go, she asked?

He watched, knowing the timing wasn't right and sighed. "We do. Now, we're playing we're on holidays. What do we do first?"

She spun, catching the flash of amusement in his eyes. "I have no idea. I have never been on holidays."

He froze, his eyes on her, shock running through him. "Never? Your parents never took you?"

She shook her head. "They went. They took Adam, but never me."

"I'm so sorry, Aideen. I didn't mean to make light of that." He reached for her hand and drew her down to a chair, sitting near her. "I need to talk to you. I wanted to put it off, but we can't. Rory heard from Dad. That photo was doctored to look more like you. They've spoken with the lady."

She nodded. "I figured that out. Now what?" She sighed. "A new theme song for us. Now what."

He laughed even as he agreed. "We'll get there. At the moment, I am taking you out for dinner. What you have on is fine. Rory says there's a neat little restaurant about five minutes from here. Up for it?"

She stared at him before she nodded. "Just let me freshen up and I'll be ready to go." She paused and turned back from the hallway. "Reilly, are you sure?"

He nodded. "I am. Go on. Go get ready."

Chapter 26

A week later, Reilly looked up from his work, hearing the happy tones in Aideen's voice and smiled. It had done her good, he thought. She was blossoming under his eyes. Occasionally, he would catch her watching him, a look he couldn't read on her face before she would look away. There had been no news on the ones after her, and that concerned him. It was only a matter of time before they found them.

He looked down at his paperwork. He had been working remotely for his father, but felt restless. He knew that wasn't what he wanted to do. He sighed. He had no idea where he was going, only the good Lord knew that, but he felt content in this town. He rose, intent on finding his wife and heading for town, or for a walk on the beach, whichever she was up to.

Aideen looked up from the garden she had been working on. Leah had been gracious, letting her work up an area around the cottage and plant it, to Aideen's delight. That had been something she had always wanted to do, garden, but had never been allowed to.

"Ready for a walk, my love?" Reilly grinned at her as she looked at him and then scowled at her hands.

"Only you would ask that when I look like this. Five minutes." She flew past him into the cottage and was as good as her word, back with him in less than that. "Where are we off to?"

"We can head into town or we can pack a lunch and head for the beach."

“The beach. I never get tired of that. Is it safe?”

Reilly shrugged. “I have no idea, but I refuse to let you live in fear any more.”

She sighed and sat on the steps, patting the wood beside her. “Sit, Reilly. We need to talk.”

“Not today. Not right now. Right now, we’re going to do something fun.” He looked up as he heard a throat clear and glared at Rory. “What do you want?”

Rory laughed, but the laugh did not meet his eyes. “Just wanted to see what you two were planning. Dad’s heading this way this afternoon.”

“What time?”

“About three, he said.”

“Okay. We’ll be back by then.” Reilly looked back at the cottage door, knowing Aideen had gone to pack a lunch for them. “We’re heading for the beach for a bit. If we’re not back by two, come looking for us.”

Rory nodded. “This sounds so familiar, Reilly. Please. Stay safe this time.”

Reilly shared a look with his brother. “I have every intention of doing just that.”

Rory looked at the clock later that day. It was almost three and he could hear his father’s voice speaking with Leah. He rose from his desk, heading for the door and the cottage. He knocked, not getting a response and tried the knob. It turned under his hand and he entered, calling for Reilly or Aideen, and finding neither. His heart dropped. They had never come back. He had been engrossed in his work and lost track of time.

He turned, running for the house, calling for his father, who stood, shock on his face and then reaching for his dress shoes, pulling them off and putting on his boots. Leah was there, a backpack for each, supplies and water in them. Rory kissed her swiftly, asking her to call for help if she hadn't heard from them in an hour. The two man ran for the path, praying the couple had just lost track of time, but knowing it was unlikely.

They searched the bay, the shoreline, the trails to the beach, finding no sign of the couple. Volunteers appeared, and the search widened. The couple had disappeared.

A day went by, and then another and another. Riordan paced the bed and breakfast, Naomi cleaned, the four siblings immersed in a search. No word came in form of a ransom note. No one had seen anything.

Just where they were, no one knew, or knew if they were even still alive. That was what drove the search. Riordan had his men fly over in a search pattern, finding nothing. He searched desperately, knowing that he needed to find them before it was too late. Nothing was found.

A week later, a man appeared in the doorway, a backpack in his hand. He asked for Riordan and then for one of the brothers.

Rory talked with him, taking the backpack, a frown on his face. There was no way it had just appeared on the beach, not with the search that had been going on. He raised his eyes to the officer standing behind the man and nodded, watching as the man was led away.

Regan appeared beside him, a frown on her face.

"What was that about?"

Rory turned, concern in his eyes. "That man? He said he found this on the beach and asked if we were looking for it."

Regan snorted. "There's no way that happened. We've searched the beach and the bay too many times." She pointed at it. "So, what's in it?"

Rory headed for the kitchen, Leah looking up and then reached for newspapers to spread out. He set the back down, a prayer in his heart, and opened it. "It's Reilly's." He dumped out the contents, feeling around for anything he might have missed.

Regan sorted through the backpack. "There's no food or water and Reilly would have had that. Just a book, which he wouldn't read, and some papers. How do we know it's his?"

Rory tilted the flap. "It's his. I remember him having it personalized." He frowned, sorting through the papers. "This papers are nonsense. Reilly wouldn't have done this. Unless...". His voice died away as he gave closer attention to the papers.

"There's nothing there, just blank. That's odd." Regan reached for the book, flipping through it. "Wait. What's this? There are underlined words."

Rory reached for it. "Leah, where's that pad of paper and pen you always keep in the kitchen? Thanks, love. Regan, start writing as I read." Rory turned back to the front of the book and carefully turned each page, the words he uttered written down by Regan.

She stared at them. "This makes no sense."

Rory shook his head. "No, they won't. It will be code of some kind." He looked around. "We need Ryanne. She's good at this. Almost as good as Reilly."

Regan nodded, turning to find their sister, pulling her with her at her protest. "Ryanne, stop. We need your help. We have a code here we need to decipher."

Ryanne paused, her eyes shifting between the two in front of her. "A code? Where did it come from?" She just shook her head when Rory explained. "This does not make sense, Rory. Who would do this?" She reached for the paper Regan and used and then the book. She frowned. "Reilly wouldn't read this."

"We know. Take a look at the paper, please?" Rory was getting frustrated even as his eyes raised to find his father standing there. "Dad?"

"What do you have?"

"A code of some kind, I think, but I'm not sure if Reilly did it or not."

"Let's see what it says."

Ryanne disappeared, taking the book and the paper with her. An hour later, they heard running footsteps and she appeared at the door, excitement in her face.

"I found them. They're on a boat near the shore."

"How?"

"Reilly didn't do this. It's not his style, but whoever left it must have. It was a simple code, almost too simple. I'll explain it later." She spun to Leah. "Is there a boat we can use?"

Leah turned from her phone. "Jordan, a friend, is on his way to the marina. Head that way. He has a larger cabin cruiser you can use." She stopped speaking her eyes on Rory. "Don't all go.

Make it seem as if you're heading out for a simple cruise or fishing or something."

Riordan grinned at her for a moment. "Excellent thinking, my dear." He searched the faces of his family, raising his eyes to study his wife, who nodded. "Okay, Rory, you stay. We need it to look as if we're tourists, right? I highly doubt you would go with a group of guests, now would you? But then you might. Okay. Rory, Redmond, Regan. Ryanne, I need you to stay here and search through that book. Make sure we didn't miss anything."

They ran to change to more casual clothes, heading for the marina, Riordan pausing for a moment beside Naomi before hugging her and heading out after his children.

Jordan, a friend of Leah's, studied the group and then took the paper Riordan handed him, a frown on his face.

"You think they're here?"

"We do. Is that a problem?"

He shook his head. "I'm just surprised. It's not that far from Leah's property. She mentioned in passing what happened." He held up a hand, stilling Riordan's comment. "You can trust me. She just asked if I could be on the lookout for a boat that didn't belong."

He set off, finally idling the cruiser near the entrance to a bay. "This is it. We'll go in. I just hope no one is around."

"You and me both." Riordan stood beside Jordan as he maneuvered the cruiser through the opening. "There. Should that be there?"

Jordan shook his head. "No. Wait. That's Old Man Baker's boat. He reported it stolen a couple of weeks ago. We haven't been able to find it. Do you think?"

Riordan nodded, his eyes on the boat and then his family. "I do think. What better way to hide them then on a local boat."

Riordan reached for the railing of the other boat, securing it to Jordan's. He paused, then turned to his family. "We pray first."

Slipping over the railing, they searched the boat, finally coming to a locked cabin. Rory reached for the knob, knowing somehow they had found them. He shoved at the door and the fragile lock broke, sending the door inwards, his grasp on the knob the only thing keeping him upright. The room was dull and it took a moment for their eyes to adjust.

Regan gave a strangled cry and then was past Rory, on her knees beside Aideen, Redmond beside Reilly.

"They're alive, Dad." Regan turned to her father. "We need to get them out of here."

Gathering up the two, they hurried from the cabin, up to the deck and then handing them over the railing to Rory and Redmond. Jordan pointed below deck, and then released the other boat, a question on Riordan's face at that.

Jordan spoke. "We leave it here. I've called for the police. They'll move in, take it into evidence and then go from there. We can't move it."

Riordan nodded. "You're right. Now, get us out of here and back to Leah's bay. We'll go in from there."

Jordan nodded himself. "I was going to suggest that. I spoke with Leah. She's having the local doctor and his wife come out on a pretense for a meal. They do that quite often. He's related to her, so no one would think anything of that."

"Well, I must say, you're ahead of me." Riordan turned, his eyes on the stairs. "I just pray we're in time. We need this over for them."

"And it will be. Don't worry. God is in control."

Chapter 27

Stirring restlessly, Reilly slowly roused, hearing soft sounds around him, not sure where he even was. He cracked his eyes open slightly and then closed them again as he heard footsteps. A hand felt his head and then his wrist, holding the wrist lightly for a moment before gently tucking it back under a cover. He tried to rouse more but sleep claimed him.

Naomi watched as the doctor stood back before he looked over at her, a smile in place.

"He's rousing, Naomi. Give him a couple of days and he'll be on his feet." Doc Major stood back before he turned for the door. "Let's go check on Aideen. She's not rousing and I need to know why."

"I think she's given up, that's why." Naomi had shared part of Aideen's story, just enough that he knew what she had faced.

Doc nodded. "That may well be. We need to get Reilly on his feet and to her."

"I don't think that will work, Doc. You see, Reilly married her to keep her safe. It was not a love match, unfortunately."

Doc shook his head. "Really? Then we'll get them on their feet, sit them down and talk turkey to them."

Naomi gave a soft laugh. "Somehow, I don't think that will work either."

She stood at Aideen's side, seeing the paleness of the younger woman's face, the dark circles, heard the shallow breathing. Doc looked up at her for a moment.

"She's starting to come around. Give her a day or so." He checked the IV and then looked past Naomi at Regan. "Regan, my dear. You're here. Good. Come, sit with Aideen for a while."

Riordan turned as Naomi touched his back and swept an arm around her. "What the news?"

"Reilly was awake for a few seconds and Doc feels Aideen is starting to come around. What did they go through, Riordan?"

"That we may never know. The police have scoured the boat and found some evidence, evidence they're not sharing." Riordan sighed, his gaze turning to his wife. "We have to head back soon, love. I'm needed at the office."

"I know. I want to stay. Take Redmond, Regan, and Ryanne with you. We'll be fine."

"I just worry. This is not that secure."

"Riordan, they've proved it doesn't matter how secure an area is. They can still get to them."

Rory watched as his father and siblings drove away the next day before his feet took him to his brother's room, where he stood for a moment before sitting, his heart raised in prayer. He looked up after a while. Reilly was awake and watching him.

"Reilly? You're awake!"

Reilly gave a brief nod. "Where am I?"

"At our place. You're safe."

Reilly stared at him and shook his head. "No, we're not. They'll be back." He shifted in bed. "Aideen?"

"She's here. Mom's with her right now." Rory studied his brother. "What happened?"

"What happened? What happened is that I tried to go for a walk with Aideen, was ambushed about the same spot as last time, taken to a boat, and then left there to die. What else would you like to know?" His bitterness came through and Rory sat back.

"Reilly? Did you get a look at them?"

Reilly shook his head. "I didn't. They knocked me out. But I heard Aideen calling someone by name. I could tell she was shocked by who she saw. Has she been able to give you that name?"

"She still sleeping a lot. We haven't questioned her yet. Doc won't let us." Rory turned to stare at the door. "Someone brought us your backpack with a book in it. It was underlined in spots, and Ryanne solved the message. Who would do that?"

Reilly stared at him before turning his gaze to the ceiling. "There was one man who really didn't seem to fit. I wonder if he was undercover."

"He may have been. We'll not likely know." Rory rose and paced. "What was the purpose of taking you?"

Reilly shrugged. "I got the impression we were taken to put pressure on someone else. Who that was, I have no idea. Is Dad around?"

"No, he had to head back. Why?"

"Because I think whoever it was knows Dad."

"Knows Dad?" Rory stared at his brother, then turned his head as he heard a sound.

"Knows your father, Reilly? Why would you say that?" Naomi sat on the edge of his bed, her eyes on her son.

He shrugged, even as he tried to keep his eyes open. "It's just an impression I have."

Rory stared at his mother before looking back at his brother. "Did he really just do that?"

"Fall asleep again?" Naomi nodded. "He did."

She rose, heading for Aideen, stopping in the doorway to study the younger woman. Aideen's head was turning and Naomi could see she was in distress. She reached for her and drew her into a hug, listening to the murmurs, her heart stopping as she heard a name. It couldn't be!

She finally rose, her eyes staring at the window before she looked for her phone.

"Riordan? I know who it is." When she gave the name, she heard the silence on the other end. "Riordan?"

"That makes it even worse. How do we tie the two families together?" Riordan was pacing, she could tell. "Leave it with me, love. We need to do some heavy research."

"I know you do. The police have been here, trying to talk to the two, but they haven't been able to. How do we keep everyone safe?"

"We're working on that. It may mean bringing you back here."

"That won't work. Leah won't leave and Rory won't leave Leah. And I know Aideen and Reilly won't want to."

Riordan sighed. "Leave it with me, then. I'll be back tomorrow."

Chapter 28

Reilly sank down in the chair by his wife's bed, his eyes on her, before he reached for her hand. It had been a week since they had been found. He had given his statement but he could tell the police were no further ahead. That frustrated him. He wanted this over. He wanted a chance to talk to Aideen, tell her how he felt, and assess whether they could go on.

He watched her face, seeing her sleeping peacefully at last. It had been a struggle, his mother had informed him, getting her to rouse and then to sleep. He knew what she wasn't saying. Aideen was giving up, thinking that she would never be free to live her life. Lord, how do we reach her?

Aideen stirred, her hand tightening on Reilly's before she moved it, rolling to her side, facing away from him as she roused, her eyes flickering open. She sighed. She wasn't on the boat, but where was she? She could hear the sound of breathing and froze, before she rolled back, her eyes on Reilly as he sat, head bowed, lost in his prayers. She watched him, her heart in her eyes before she smothered it. She couldn't let him know she cared. She had to make him think she didn't.

She looked around, liking what she saw, but knowing as soon as she was on her feet, she would leave. She had brought danger to his family and that she had to end, even if it meant with her own life.

Reilly raised his head, his eyes on her as she stared back at him.

"Aideen? Oh, my love, you're awake!" He sat, a frown on his face, sensing she didn't want him near her. "Aideen? Are you okay?"

She shook her head. "No, Reilly, I'm not. I can't do this any more." She rolled away from him, her arm covering her face, fighting back tears.

Reilly rose, determination on his face. He would not let her be hurt any more. He searched and found his father, waiting until he looked up, before he spoke. Riordan hesitated and then nodded, agreeing with Reilly's plan. His heart broke for his son, knowing that he was willing to put himself out there, willing to die if necessary. That was who he was, Riordan knew.

Redmond shook his head. "There is no way that will work, Reilly."

"And why won't it? What else can we do?"

Redmond stared at him. "You really mean this, don't you?"

Reilly nodded. "I know of no other way to do this. Mom heard her say the name. I've talked to Dad. He's not sure if the man is in the area, but I know he is. He would have waited for us to be found. That was his plan all along. He's trying to break Aideen. I won't let that happen."

He walked away, to the outdoors and then to town, letting himself be seen, asking if the man Aideen named had been seen in town. The townsfolk stared at him and then shook their heads. A couple hesitated but then said nothing.

Reilly finally walked back towards the bed and breakfast, stopping to watch the families on the beach, before he sighed and walked towards the water. He needed to go to Aideen but he sensed she needed some time. How much time he gave her, he just wasn't sure.

He finally walked into the kitchen, searching for his family, not seeing them and frowning. He headed for Aideen, stopping to watch as she sat up in a chair, knowing she was too weak for that. He perched on the edge of the bed, not saying anything, waiting for her to speak.

"Aideen?"

She turned, her eyes shadowed. "Reilly, what am I to do with you? You can't put yourself out there."

"Too late, Aideen. I already have. I need to do this. I need to make sure you're safe. How else can I do that?" He reached for her hands, rubbing his thumbs along her fingers. "It's just, my love, that I can't bear to think of anything more happening to you."

She just sat, not responding, before she sighed. "God is in control, you know. Not you. Not me. Did you pray and really pray about this?"

He nodded. "I did, my love. I want this over for you."

She sighed, withdrawing her hands and wrapping them in the blanket she had on her knee. "Your dad asked me about that name. I don't remember saying it."

"Mom said you kept repeating it before you awakened. How do you know him?"

She shrugged. "I don't remember. I think he was a partner or in business with my father." She looked up. "Does it never end?"

"It will. We're working towards that end." He paused as he heard a noise from the hallway and rose, stopping in shock as he saw his father standing there, a gun to his head. "Dad?"

"Reilly, I need you and Aideen to come out here, please. Carefully."

Reilly felt Aideen's hand on his arm and reached for it, not taking his eyes from his father. He heard the sharply indrawn breath Aideen gave and knew that this was it. Someone would not be walking away from this, he knew.

He walked them towards his father, watching as Riordan was backed away from them. He looked for rest of his family, not seeing them, seeing instead the hard look in his father's eye, one he had never seen before. This is not good, he thought.

He sat on the chair he was directed to, Aideen on the arm of his chair, his hand still holding hers tight. He waited, not sure what for. Riordan was forced to his knees in front of them, the gun still trained on him, his hands locked behind his neck. He gave a slight head shake at Reilly.

"Where are the others, Dad?" Reilly had to ask. He felt the blow against the back of his head, not realizing someone stood behind him.

Aideen gave a small scream, clapping her free hand over her mouth. Her eyes were on the doorway behind Riordan, her hand tightening on Reilly.

"He's here, Reilly. Oh, dear Lord, protect us."

Reilly shifted slightly so he could watch her face, before he looked at the doorway, a frown in place. He knew the man but it wasn't the name Aideen had given him.

"Theodore? What is going on?" Reilly spoke, not realizing that he had.

Riordan's eyes slid closed. Reilly had just confirmed his suspicions, suspicions that he had been working through and had not had a chance to pass on to the investigators. He regretted that. He had no idea where the rest of his family were, just that they had been separated.

Redmond stared at the door, closed and locked to the storeroom before he tried to open it.

"That's not going to work, Redmond." Rory stood beside him, searching. "There has to be another way. Leah?" He turned, finding Leah already searching the wall behind her. "Is there another way out?"

"There is. I just have to find it." She heard a click. "Here. If we slid this away, it should be a way out."

Rory was at her side, brushing aside the cobwebs and peering in to the opening. "All right, here we go. I'll go first, you ladies next, and Redmond at the rear. Can he close the opening from inside?"

Leah had been studying the opening. "He can. Redmond, push this. It will close it." She turned, her eyes on the rest. "I am so glad this house has all these secret passages. They do come in handy."

Rory paused as he came to the outside of the house, his hand up, watching and listening. "They must all be inside." His voice was a mere whisper. "Ladies, head for town. Regan. You're with us. Ryanne, stay with Mom and Leah."

They nodded and separated, Redmond and Regan watching Rory closely. He knew the house, knew how to get them in and out safely.

"What now, Rory?" Redmond stood at his shoulder, watching.

"It's up to us. Regan, head for the other side of the house. Be careful. We know there are four of them. I have no idea how many will be with Dad, Reilly and Aideen."

"Likely all of them. Theodore is very arrogant. He always has been. He won't think we can get away."

Rory nodded and then watched as she slipped away. He pointed to himself and the back door. Redmond nodded and headed away from him, towards the side of the house and the French doors that opened into the living room. He paused as he watched, seeing the three together. Regan was right. All four men were there. He frowned as he saw his father on his knees and then realized that was done on purpose. Theodore was trying to get the upper hand and this was one way he thought he could.

He caught a brief view of Rory in the far doorway before he stepped out of sight. He watched closely, unable to hear what was being said, but seeing the agitation in the older man, knew they had to come up with a plan and quickly. He started as he heard a sound and then felt a hand on his shoulder before Rory's voice whispered in his ear.

"Regan found one of the man and took him out. That leaves those three."

"And those three are the ones we have to worry about. Wait, what's that one doing?"

"He's heading for the kitchen. Wait here." Rory was gone and then back before Redmond could respond.

"Did you get him?"

"I did. I locked him into the pantry. Leah's going to have my head, you know." Rory watched closely. "We're going to have to move in soon. But how?"

Redmond looked around and then took another look. "Regan's in there. I can see her in the shadows."

"I see that. Now, how do we get in?"

"The windows in the bedroom. Can we go through them?"

Rory thought and then nodded. "They're open and the screens will come out. Come on. I don't think we have much time."

Chapter 29

Reilly watched closely as his father spoke with Theodore, trying to determine just how the families had intersected with one another. He felt Aideen leaning on him and gave a quick look up. He frowned at the look on her face, not sure what she was up to, but sure she had a plan. She wasn't strong enough to do anything, though, he thought.

He glimpsed Regan briefly in the shadows before she moved back. Good, he thought. They've gotten out. That means Redmond and Rory are around somewhere. Ryanne has likely taken off with Leah and Mom. At least, I hope that's how it went down. They'll head for help.

He jumped at a sudden noise, feeling Aideen gripping his hand tighter, before she looked around.

"What was that?" Aideen had just the right touch of fear in her voice, but Reilly knew she wasn't afraid. Not of the man in front of her.

"Nothing for you to be concerned about, my dear." Theodore stopped in front of her, his hand stroking down her hair. "You were to be my daughter-in-law, you know. Until Adam was killed and my son with him."

"Your son? And who would that be? And just why was Adam killed?" She was taunting him, buying time for them but also trying to find answers.

"Adam knew too much. He found paperwork that showed my dealings with contacts overseas and how they wanted to infiltrate the savings companies here. We were working that way, until you found that paperwork and turned it in."

"And just how would you know that?"

"Your lawyer. He contacted me and let me know."

Aideen shook her head. "I have no lawyer. I only spoke with the prosecutor. So again, how did you know?" She was pushing and Reilly wished she wouldn't, but knew why she was.

"He was. He said he was. He was Aton Jones."

She stared at him. "That was Adam's lawyer. Adam played you and played you well. Everything was a game to him, one he was determined to win at all costs. I know. I felt the brunt of it all my life."

Theodore shook his head. "No, he was your lawyer."

She shook her head again, a look of pity on her face. "Sorry, not my lawyer. I just don't get it. How do you connect with the Stuarts?"

"I can tell you, Aideen." Riordan spoke up, knowing she was trying to put in time until the authorities could get there. "He wanted to invest in our company, wanted all kinds of financial information. I refused to let him have that. In fact, at one point, I had to have him escorted off the premises."

Theodore spent to stare at Riordan. "And for that, I will never forgive you. I wanted to invest in your company, yes. It was the perfect cover for my monies. No one would have guessed."

Riordan shook his head, sadness on his face. "They would have. We don't do the accounting ourselves. You didn't know that, did you? We have a company that looks after that, and they do a forensics audit every year. You would never have succeeded, no matter how you tried." He paused, his eyes on

Reilly. "But that doesn't explain why you went after Aideen or Reilly?"

"Reilly got in my way, plain and simple. I wanted him out of the way. When my son was killed I wanted you to suffer to. I wanted one of your sons to die." He began to ramble, his words not coherent or logical.

Reilly stared at his father, a frown on his face. What had just happened?

Theodore snapped out of whatever state he had drifted to, his eyes on Aideen, real hatred in them. He reached and pulled her to her feet, her wrist tight in his. She struggled, unable to free herself. Reilly had started to rise but felt the hand on his shoulder, sagging back into this seat, watching for something he could do. He heard the barest whisper of sound in the house, not sure what it was.

Aideen finally twisted her arm enough she could break contact with Theodore. She shoved at him, sending him away from her, before she threw herself to the floor, calling for Riordan and Reilly to do the same. Both men dove for the floor, hearing shouts above them and the sound of running, heavy footsteps. A hand on her back had Aideen scurrying sideways until she looked up into the face of a uniformed officer who helped her to her feet. She turned, spying Reilly and was across the room and in his arms, her arms tight around his neck.

Reilly buried his head against her before he swept her into his arms and turned for the outdoors, armed officers around them. Riordan was on their heels, searching for his family, finding his two sons and Regan waiting for him.

"Your Mom? Ryanne? Leah?"

"They're safe, Dad. We sent them to town and they sent help. We'll find them soon." Rory looked up. "We'll need to do something about our guests. Leah will look after that. We should be able to open up again by teatime, I'm told."

Riordan hugged his three children before he turned to Reilly and Aideen, his arms coming around the couple as he prayed, tears on his face.

Aideen stared at the house, watching the activity. "It's over?"

"It is, all but the mopping up as they say." Reilly watched as well. "I never knew that about him, Dad. Was he always like that?"

"I fear he was. None of us had a good feeling about him. There was always something about him that kept us from getting too close to him." He sighed. "I'm sorry, Aideen. I am really sorry."

"For what? You didn't cause him to be like he was. Sin did that." She slid from Reilly's arm and began to pace, until her steps faltered and he swept her back into his arms. "Is it really over?"

Reilly nodded, sorrow briefly crossing his face. "It is. Dad will find out what else there is to know." He looked up as a senior officer walked their way.

"I'm sorry, Rory. I wish I could have prevent this." Joe Storme looked at Rory. "You and Leah have had enough, without this. He's been around town, trying to invest in businesses, but from what I'm told no one would accept his money. Is it Aideen?" At her nod, he continued. "He's confessed to killing your brother and your parents. Rage and jealousy is why. He did say that he knew they hadn't wanted you and that was why he was trying to get you to marry his son."

"I have no idea who his son was. I stayed away from all my brother's friends. Even on the run,

I did that." She leaned back against Reilly. "Can we go home now?"

Joe Storme laughed, and then spoke. "In a while. We'll need to get your statements. We have some issues to work through but that's our problem not yours. You can leave a number for us and we'll be in touch." Shaking their hands, he walked away, heading for his officers.

Riordan watched for a moment before he spoke. "I suspect we'll have a lot of questions we'll need to answer but it's over. Theodore would have been behind everything you two went through. This bit with the boat? I can see him doing that for spite, leaving you two to die, letting us grieve because you were lost." He turned to his family. "Let's head into town and find the rest of our group. Aideen, are you up for it?"

She hesitated, knowing that she wasn't before Rory spoke. "We have an old-fashioned wheelchair in the garage, Dad. Just the thing for Aideen." He grinned at her frown, feeling the release of worry and stress.

Chapter 30

Over the following few weeks, it became clearer what the motivation was. Theodore Whyte had wanted to set up an empire for himself. Aideen's mother was a distant cousin and he saw in her husband the ideal fall guy. Aideen never knew that he had been related to her, just knew she didn't like him, didn't want to be around him and when she could run from her family she had ran as far as she could. Only Adam hadn't let her. He had tracked her, tried to destroy her, and had ultimately paid with his life for that. Theodore had been aware of what he was doing and had finally decided to take Aideen's family out of the way, thinking she would run to him for help. When Reilly stepped in to help her, he became a target. Everything they had undergone had been at the hands of the monster as Aideen described him.

Trials would take place but it would take time. Medical evidence revealed that Theodore had mental issues, had always had them but had hidden them. The lifestyle he lived had aggravated that to the point there were times he was totally unaware of what he was doing.

Reilly watched as Aideen grew thin, the stress driving her to wander the house at night, unable to sleep. She refused to talk to him. Dark shadows lined her pale face. He wanted to make it better for her but had no idea how to. He had talked to his father, who could give him little advice, other than to pray.

He watched her one day, seeing her sitting, arms wrapped around her legs, her head laying on the back of the couch, her eyes on the window. A shuttered look covered her face. He sighed and rose. There was only one thing he could think of that might help. He stood for a moment before he stooped and dropped a kiss on her hair, walking towards the bedroom he used. He paused, turning so he could watch her, and then resolute in his determination, walked forward, pulling out his duffel bags and packing. He had done what he said he would do. He had kept her safe, gotten her through the danger, and now he had to set her free. By the time he returned to the kitchen, she was gone.

He looked down at his ring and pulled it from his finger, leaving it on the table. He picked up his bags and walked away, shutting the door quietly behind him. He had one last task to do before he left town. He had asked for a leave of absence from work. His parents had studied him and then agreed, knowing he needed time with God and that time had to be on his own. They only asked he leave an address with him. He scrawled it on a paper and threw it on the desk, walking away.

He opened the door to the house quietly once more, finding Aideen standing in the kitchen, her eyes on him, a question on her face. He paused before he handed her the large legal sized envelope.

"Aideen, I said I would keep you safe and get you through what you were facing. And I promised to set you free once that was done." He looked down, a stern look coming to his face, fighting back his emotions before he looked up again. "These are the annulment papers I promised you. I've signed them. You just need to sign them. The lawyer's information is on the first sheet."

When she refused to take them, he laid them down, hesitated for a moment, and then turned and walked away, not looking at her, not seeing the devastation his actions had brought. She ran after him, too late she saw as he drove away. She dropped to the floor in a huddle, her sobs shuddering through her body.

She didn't feel the hands on her arms, drawing her to her feet, or the mother's arm that held her tight, or the father's arms that surrounded the two women. She heard the prayer and finally looked up at Naomi and Riordan.

"Why? Why did he walk away?" She looked down at his ring she had on her finger. "I didn't want him to."

"We know, dear. You love him. And he loves you to the point he will set you free, to let you live a life you have never been able to. That's who Reilly is. He wouldn't say anything and feel that he had trapped you into staying with him." Naomi drew Aideen down beside her on the couch, hearing Riordan moving around in the kitchen. "What do you want to do?"

Aideen shrugged. "I don't want him to leave. I need him." She looked up at the ceiling, tears blinding her. "I love him, Naomi. I love him so much."

"We know, dear. We know. We saw. But you couldn't say anything before. But now you can. He has released you. It's up to you if you take the release or not."

"I don't understand."

Riordan set the tray he was carrying down and then sat beside her, reaching for her hand. "I'm going to talk to you just like I would one of my girls. I think of you as that. Reilly is an honourable man. He would not keep you in a marriage he felt trapped you. He would let you go. It is up to you whether that happens or not. You can go to him and tell him how you feel or we can make some plans and bring him back to you."

"Plans?"

Reilly's parents each took a turn speaking with her. She turned to watch and then stood, moving towards the kitchen and picking up the envelope.

"First things first. I need to take care of this." She looked up as Naomi approached her.

"Good for you. When you're done that, come find me. No. That won't work. I'm going with you and then we're going shopping. This is going to be fun."

Riordan shook his head at his wife. "You just want an excuse to shop. Aideen, I'll take care of my part. How long do you think?"

"A week? Is that too soon?"

Naomi shook her head. "Not soon enough, but we need time to plan. We'll get him back here, even if we have to hogtie him and drag him back."

Aideen stared at her, shocked, and then heard Riordan laughing as Naomi swept her out of the house.

Aideen walked into the lawyer's office, left the envelope and walked out, leaving the lawyer staring after her, with a promise not to contact Reilly for ten days. He shook his head and without comment, set the envelope on his desk. He left, needing to find his own wife. Things were confusing, and he needed her advice.

Reilly stared at Rory a week later.

"What do you mean, a family meeting? Dad would have called."

"He's been trying. Check your phone. He says it's going right voice mail." Rory straightened his suit jacket, not wanting to give anything away. "And he says it's a formal meeting, so go and get your suit on."

Reilly glared at his brother before he walked away. What was his father up to, he wondered? They had family meetings but never one where they had to dress up.

He watched as Rory parked and then hesitated before he slid from behind the wheel, waiting for Reilly to follow him.

Reilly's hand stopped his brother. "Rory, what is really going on?"

Rory looked at him before looking over his head. "It's a family meeting. That's all I know. Dad wants all of us there. He hasn't said much."

Reilly nodded, knowing his father could sometimes pull something like this. "Is Aideen here?"

"I have no idea. I dropped Leah off and then was sent to find you. So I have no idea who's all here. Does it matter if she is?"

Reilly paused, then shook his head, not letting his brother see his face. Rory's heart broke for his brother. They had talked, these two men, and Reilly had told him that he had given Aideen the annulment papers he had promised her. Rory knew just how much that hurt Reilly. He had seen the tears Reilly wouldn't shed. He had seen the desperation in Reilly to keep his lady safe, even if it meant he had to walk away.

Reilly greeted his family and then looked around, a frown on his face. Something was up and he wasn't sure what. He turned as he heard heels tapping on the floor behind him and stopped at the vision in front of him. Aideen? And in a white wedding dress? What was going on?

Aideen drew a deep breath. She had put it all on the line for this moment and suddenly she was afraid, afraid that her love was not returned despite reassurances to the contrary, afraid that Reilly would walk away from her, leaving her standing once more watching him.

"Aideen?" His voice was barely a whisper.

"Reilly, you walked away from me a week ago, leaving me with the papers you promised. You kept your promise. You kept me as safe as you could. You put your life on the line to do that. You asked for nothing from me, other than that I trust you. A week ago, you gave me what you thought I wanted, my freedom." She had to pause, biting at her lip.

"Aideen?" His whisper reached to her heart.

"Reilly, I don't want my freedom. I love you too much. I just don't know if you love me back. I think you do. I'm told you do. But I need to hear it from you. And if you can't, then that's okay." Tears glistened in her eyes. When he didn't speak, she swallowed hard and turned away, ready to walk away.

"Aideen, please. Don't walk away." Reilly's feet took him to stand just behind her. "I love you. You're the other half of my heart. I couldn't stay here and see you, thinking you didn't love me." His hands reached for her arms, turning her to face him. "Please, don't walk away. My heart can't take it."

She searched his face and then was in his arms, her veil crushed against her as he held her, tears shaking both their bodies. Riordan finally moved to them, his arms around them, his prayer reaching through their emotions.

"Reilly. Aideen. The pastor's here. If you want to go ahead with your plans, Aideen, now's the time."

Reilly stared at his father and then at Aideen. "There's no family meeting, is there, Dad?"

Riordan grinned, looking very much like his son. "Oh, but there is. The best kind of family meeting. We get to watch you two redo your vows. We missed the first one. This time, your family's here. Aideen, we have welcomed you into our home. You have become the other daughter we needed to fill our home."

Reilly searched Aideen's face. "You are beautiful. Who worked with you on this? Mom and Dad, I suspect."

"They did, Reilly." She took his hand, knowing she was loved by a good, Godly man.

Chapter 31

Aideen was on a search. She wanted to talk to Reilly about plans they were making for a vacation but she just could not find him. She stood in the living room of the house they had been renting, looking around. She loved this house but knew it had been put up for sale. She would miss it, she knew.

She searched the house and then the outside, not finding him. Then she turned, heading for the back of the yard and the path to the beach. The house was in the same town as Rory and Leah, but had beach access. She finally stopped, seeing Reilly sitting on the rock he claimed as his own. She watching for a moment, watching the setting sun playing across him, before she walked towards him, and into his arms, leaning against him.

"Reilly, I was looking for you. Do you have word when we need to move? I see the sold sticker on the sign."

He looked up at her, seeing the woman he loved more each day, and saw the worry on her face. He hugged her to him.

"We don't."

"We don't? Of course we do. There are new owners. They'll want their house."

"We don't have to move. I know the owners and we can stay." A glint of mischief peeked out of his eyes.

"You do? We can?" Aideen was trying to determine what he was meaning. "Just what do you mean?"

"Just what I said. We don't have to move."
He finally took pity on her and stood, his arm around
her as he turned her back to the house, walking in
silence until they were standing in the room he used
as an office. He picked up paperwork and handed it
to her, not saying a word.

She stared at him and then down at the
paperwork. "Reilly, this can't be right. It says we're
the owners. I never signed anything."

"Not yet. The agent's willing to have you
come in and sign. That's all it will take. The house is
ours, my love. We don't have to move." He watched
as it dawned on her.

"You bought it? But what about your work?
You'd have to commute and you don' like that."

"No, I don't have to. I can work from here
most days. And when I have to go in, you can come
to. Dad's said he wants you to work for him as well."

"He does? But what would I do?" She was
confused.

"He'll figure it out. He always does." Reilly
swept her into a hug. "So, Mrs. Stuart, is this place
acceptable to you?"

"Stuart, you're pushing it again, you know."
She leaned back to look at him. "But I love it, most
of the time, when you push. You push me to be a
better person."

"God pushes me all the time, my love. I have
to live the way He wants me to. I just pray I don't
push you too much."

She shook her head. "You don't." She
stepped away from him. "The trials start soon, don't
they?"

"They do, but we don't have a lot to do. Most of the men have taken a plea deal. I talked to the prosecutor today. He doesn't think Theodore will make it to trial. His mental condition has deteriorated that much. He's not aware of where he is or what's going on around him, not any more."

"He'll face a higher judge than here on earth at some point." She dropped into the desk chair, a finger running along the edge of the desk. "What would have happened if your family hadn't found us on that boat?"

Reilly sat on the corner of the desk, his hands clasped, his eyes on her. "We wouldn't be here, I know that. I almost lost you that day." He looked around as the doorbell rang. "Are we expecting anyone?"

"Not that I know of." She listened as Reilly answered the door, hearing a sound from him that she didn't understand. She looked up in fear as he was shoved towards her, catching himself on the desk, before he spun to face the man standing in the doorway.

Aideen stared at the man in fear. "Dad? You're dead."

"No, I'm not. That was my twin. We look enough alike that they never questioned if it was me. I left my identification on him." He strode towards her, grasping her arm and pulling her away from Reilly. "You will pay, my dear. You thwarted my plans."

"Your plans?" She didn't know what he was saying.

"That's right. You thought all along it was that slob, Theodore, that it was his plans. They were mine. I wanted my millions and then I could move away, leaving your mother and brother and you behind." He shook her. "Now, I had to come up with another plan. Reilly's parents will pay to free him. I have sent a ransom note to them."

He turned from her and paced, mumbling as he did so. Aideen reached for Reilly, her hands cold in his. Reilly wrapped her in his arms and watched, waiting for an opportunity to get her out of the room. It would come but he just didn't know when.

Hours passed as they waited, with her father becoming more and more agitated as time went by. Aideen had sat in the office chair, her eyes watching her father, waiting for what she wasn't sure. Reilly watched as well, knowing it would be up to him to take Aideen's father down, if he could.

Then the opportunity came that he had been waiting for. Her father moved closer to him, his eyes on the door, thinking he had heard a sound. Reilly was on him, taking him to the floor. Aideen was there as well, the scarf she had dropped on the desk in her hands, helping to bind her father's arms behind him. Reilly rose, scooping her into his arms and then out the door, meeting the officers heading their way.

Riordan watched from the sidelines, finally able to make his way to his family. He wrapped them in his arms and then pulled them into his car. A few words with an officer and he drove away, taking them to safety. Is it finally over, Lord, he asked? Can these two go on with their lives?

Shock ran through the family as Reilly explained what had happened and who had taken them captive. There would be questions, they knew, about the investigation and at some time, it may well be explained to them. At the moment, they were just glad the two were safe and back with them.

Epilogue

A year later, Reilly stood and watched as Aideen moved among his family. She had made herself a place there, he could see. He was glad. She had not had the family life he had and that grieved him. He turned as he felt a hand on his shoulder. Riordan stood there.

"You two have certainly had an adventure. Now that the trials are over, what are your plans?"

Reilly shrugged. "I want to take Aideen somewhere she's never been, if I can. Maybe the Maritimes."

"That sounds like a plan." Riordan handed Reilly an envelope. "I thought you might. Forgive me if I overstepped. Here are tickets for a flight down there."

"Dad? You've done enough."

"Never enough for you two. You two have shown what strong characters you are and how your love for one another is stronger day by day. Neither one of you lost your faith in God and that says a lot."

"Thanks, Dad, I guess. I need to talk to Aideen." He watched as his father walked away, heading for his mother.

Aideen looked up at that point and smiled, moving towards him.

"Reilly, are you okay? You have a look on your face that's hard to describe."

He smiled at her. "Have I told you today that I love you?" She nodded, knowing he wasn't finished speaking. "Dad just handed me tickets to fly east."

"East? As in the Maritimes? Oh, how lovely! I've always wanted to go there." She hugged him. "You have a wonderful family. I used to want to die, just to get away from mine. But if I had, I wouldn't have met you. I wouldn't be able to work at the shelter, helping those ladies and girls."

"No, God led you through so much, preparing you for what you're doing now. We don't know the reasons why He does, but He always has a plan for us. I felt for so long that we were caught on the edge of a storm, ready to be sucked in and destroyed. He prevented that."

She hugged him tighter. "That is so true. Now, when do we leave?"

He laughed. "Not yet." He opened the ticket. "Dad, you shouldn't have."

"What did he do?" She peeked at them. "First class and all. Your father is so wonderful."

"He is." Reilly watched his family, thankful to be there, but a sense of fear washed over him as he watched his three younger siblings. Lord, if it be Your will, spare them an adventure. If not, prepare them and go through it with them.

Aideen watched Reilly and knew what he was thinking. She hesitated to say anything, content just to be held and know that she was loved.

Dear Readers:

Thank you for picking up the story of Reilly and Aideen, who are caught on the edge of a storm not of their making. Their trust in God is shaken, their trust in one another shaken, their trust in others shaken. But they came through their storm and adventure, stronger and more in love with one another.

What storm are you facing? Storms take many shapes and forms. Some are physical. Some are emotional. Many are spiritual as we are in a battle every day. God has equipped us to face this and never ever leaves our side, never leaves us defenseless. That you can depend on.

My storm in recent weeks has been the health of my beloved Sheltie, Emma. It was a storm I had to go through. I lost her during the writing of this book. She had developed a tumour and kidney failure. As much as I hated to, I had to release her. God was good. He let me have time with her and then has given me peace in this storm that He was with me and that He cared about me and my pets.

Whatever storm you face, keep your eye on the One who calms them, who has you in the hollow of His hand, and covers you there. Never fear to walk with Him.

God bless each and every one of you.

Ronna